ALSO BY AUTHOR

About the Boy
Apocalypse Still

Between Us

Leah Nicole Whitcomb

Starclay Publishing

Book Cover Illustrated by Govi

Book Cover Design by Leah Nicole Whitcomb

Library of Congress Control Number: 2025918002

ISBN: 979-8-9899368-4-7 (trade paperback)

ISBN: 979-8-9899368-5-4 (ebook)

Printed in the United States of America

For Claudia, Myeshia, and Carmen
For the girls and the gays

Mixtape

Chapter One

Naima

Prom. The single most important day in a teenager's life or so they say. I always imagined spending this day getting ready with my best friend Luna. We'd wear matching dresses, and she'd put her makeup skills to use to make me look magical. Luna's here. She's working on my eye shadow now, but so is Dixie.

Dixie Davis is my other best friend Sam's girlfriend. They're both TikTok creators although it seems like Dixie is siphoning Sam's followers. There's nothing particularly bad about her. She's a pretty girl, long brown hair, thin—it sounds like I'm describing a horse.

She's not bad, really. I just, I don't know. She's trying to tell us about some beef she has with another creator that I don't care about, and I'm trying to be nice. Say my "um hmms" and "yeah" at the right time, but this is supposed to be exciting. I'm supposed to be getting ready to dance the night away with

Luna and enjoy our Saturday night, but instead we have to babysit Dixie.

"She's totally copying my style. I started the Y2K trend then she hopped on. I thought about dying my hair platinum blonde, then she went ahead and did it!" Dixie spreads herself out on my bed. For someone who cares about her looks, she doesn't care that she's wrinkling her dress. "It's like I can't win."

"It's like I don't care," I mumble to Luna who snickers.

"Hold still, I'm almost done," Luna whispers, then says to Dixie. "Girl, have you tried calling her out?"

Dixie springs up from the bed. "That's it! Everyone will know what a snake she is. Oh my god, Luna. You're the best."

"I know," Luna says while she finishes blending my smoky eye. When she's done, she moves out of the way for me to see myself in the mirror. I usually stray away from heavy eye makeup (because I don't know how to do it myself), but Luna *is* the best, and my brown eyes really pop. The rest of my makeup too, but I can't stop looking at my eyes and eyebrows. When she does my eyebrows, they look like twins. When I do them, they look like strangers.

"Luna" —I grab her hands— "I look amazing. How are you so great at everything?"

"I'm just naturally talented."

"You are!" I squeeze her and refuse to let go.

In two months, Luna is moving back to Mexico with her

family, and I'll never see her again. Okay, maybe that's being dramatic. I will see her again. I can always video call her, but she won't be a fifteen minute drive away. We won't be able to spend the night at each other's house without a long flight. She can't help me get ready for major life events and do my makeup and make me look pretty.

"You can let go now," Luna says, straining from the pressure of my hug.

"I'm sorry. Who knows how long I'll get to hug you and—" My eyes start to water. Luna has been my best friend since the fifth grade when she moved here, and now she's leaving eight years later. Sure, I may have Sam—who's undecided about moving to Los Angeles with Dixie, and my boyfriend Kamron who decided to take a gap year, but Luna is everything. She's my everything.

Luna grabs a tissue and dots my eyes. "You better not mess up my makeup, girl. Two months is plenty of time. You have plenty of time with me."

I nod and swallow the tears building up in my throat. I have plenty of time left with Luna. Two months seem like so little, but we can make it plenty.

Luna unzips her garment bag and slides into her gown. I grab my dress from my closet and step into it, pulling it up over my body. Usually, we coordinate our outfits, but I saw the perfect dress over the summer and bought it without knowing the theme for prom. The theme is Old Hollywood, and Luna used Megan Thee Stallion's Old Hollywood Met Gala look for inspiration. She's wearing a red sequin gown and has jumbo rollers in her hair. I saw this perfect teal and mint ombre tulle gown that I had to get so instead of matching with my best friend, I'm coordinating with my boyfriend. Where is he, by the way?

I grab my phone. He texted that he was on his way eleven minutes ago, so he should be here at any moment. I'm dressed. My makeup is done. My hair is a wash and go with a side part. I grab my gloves and shoes, and now I'm ready for prom.

Car doors slam outside so I look out the window and see Sam's burgundy Jeep, Kamron's white Prius, and Marcus's yellow Camaro. Kamron is leaning against his car in his black suit, and he looks so pretty with his hair braided like that. I smile remembering my first thoughts of him: pretty but annoying. A little too much of a golden boy, but I was definitely projecting. He's smart, thoughtful, patient, and yes, very pretty. I can't believe he's mine.

"Our dates are here!" I yell even though the girls are right beside me.

"Darius is gonna get on my nerves," Luna groans. "I don't know why I agreed to go with him."

"You could've been my date," I remind her.

"And what about your boyfriend? I don't want to be a third wheel."

"He'd be fine." I wave her concern away.

"I just wish Ricky wasn't an ass."

Ricky was her on again off again situationship. He never officially said they were dating, but he hated the idea of her dating anybody else. He's also twenty-two. Even though Luna is eighteen and their being together is technically legal, it doesn't make it right in my book. I say good riddance, but Luna's determined to make it work.

"Don't worry about Ricky. Worry about us tonight at prom. Just two hot girls having a very fun night."

"We're gonna have so much fun!" Dixie chimes in, and I stifle the growl in my throat.

I forgot she's still here.

As we head downstairs, Mom stops us on the stairway. Her eyes are already teary, and heat flushes my face. She's been doing this a lot lately. Every big senior year moment, there Mom is with her phone and her tears. I get it. I'm a big girl now, but it's kind of embarrassing.

"Let me get one pic of you girls before you leave?" she asks.

We stagger ourselves on the staircase and smile at her phone. "All three of you look lovely. I hope you have fun."

"Thanks Mom," I say then hug her.

She breaks away from the hug and stares at me. My chest prickles from her gaze. "Stay out as long as you like and have fun tonight, okay?"

"Yes, I know."

"I mean it. I better not see you home til midnight. Enjoy

yourself."

"I got it, Mom." I slip from her embrace and head for the door. Although she's putting a lot of emphasis on tonight, I secretly hope that prom is as good as its promise.

Chapter Two

Kamron

The first time I saw Naima was in our high school cafeteria. She had these bright green locs and was yelling "whore" at a white boy. I didn't know who that girl was but knew that she was kinda bold and real for that. Then I saw her again in my next class and learned that she's brilliant, and it doesn't take a genius to see how beautiful she is.

Bold. Brilliant. Beautiful. The girl I'm lucky to call my girlfriend.

When she opens the door and walks out, she's glowing. Her hair radiates from her head in a coily crown. Her dress curves in and flairs out. With the gloves on, she looks better than Princess Tiana. Better than all the Disney princesses combined, and when she smiles, my heart beats so loud in my chest that I think I may be having a heart attack.

Naima wraps her arms around my waist with a cloud of vanilla perfuming the air. She looks at me, expecting me to say something, but when I open my mouth, nothing comes out. What can I say? After all this time, I'm still astounded by the fact that this bold, beautiful, brilliant girl wants to be with me. I have no choice but to be honest with her about it.

"I have no words to describe how beautiful you are, baby."

Her smile widens to the point that her eyes squint and her face is just teeth and lashes. She grabs my face and kisses me.

"I think you can come up with just a few words," she whispers but her voice is always soft-spoken.

Her gaze travels from my lips to my eyes. I gulp. 'Stunning' is too simple.

"Glamorous? Magnificent? Alluring?"

She visibly shivers when I say each word. "I'll take all of them."

Now, I'm smiling because of course there's so many wonderful words that can describe her at one time.

"Can you two quit being gross so we can go?" Luna says.

I slick forgot other people were around. Every moment with Naima is like being tucked away in our own little cocoon. The rest of the world doesn't matter. Looking outside our cocoon though, Luna, Darius, Sam, Dixie, Marcus, and Sophie are all staring at us. Apologetically, I look from them to Naima and follow everyone to our cars. Everybody wants to carpool, but I know Naima will get tired early, and when she's tired, she's cranky so I decide that we go in my car and follow everyone else.

When we get to the convention center, the parking lot is filled with limos. An actual red carpet leads into the building, and there are photographers taking everyone's pictures like paparazzi. They don't play about prom down here. Naima rushes out of the car and runs to Luna so they can get their pictures taken. They pose, hug, and hold hands on the red carpet being ushered along by the incoming couples. Once they reach the entrance, Naima ducks under the rope and runs towards me. She grabs my hand to follow her to the start of the red carpet.

It's disorienting having the cameras flash in my face and not knowing where to look, but when I look over at Naima, she's eating it up. She's tilting her face and putting her hands on her hips. She's naturally photogenic, so I follow her lead and wrap my arm a little tighter around her waist and smile so I don't ruin her photos. When we reach the entrance, I want to breathe a sigh of relief until she goes back under the rope and grabs Sam's and Darius's hands to make everyone join us for a group photo.

And we go through the line again. This time once we're inside, Naima asks a classmate to take a picture of everyone and then she hands the phone to Luna to take a picture of the two of us. I smile at the camera before looking over at Naima. I'm at my senior prom with my girlfriend of twenty months in Mississippi. When I started high school, I didn't think any of those things could come true, but here I am. Here we are.

"What?" she says when she realizes I'm staring at her.

"I'm happy I'm here with you," I whisper near her ear, and I mean it. I never imagined I'd have the life that I have now.

Luna hands Naima her phone back, and she swipes through the photos faster than I can even process it. Eventually, she shows me one and says, "How are you so cute? You look so much better than me."

My suit's a statement piece—black with mint and teal florals that match Naima's mint and teal dress. My aunt Amaya braided my hair into this cornrow design that feeds into a bun, and she trimmed my sides. My shoes are velvet tuxedos. I clean up okay.

The girls have already picked a table near the back wall, and I follow Naima there to sit. After about ten minutes, the rest of the group joins us right as the servers bring salad and drinks. Everyone's quietly pecking at their salad until Darius asks, "What y'all doing after this?"

"Mom told me to stay out til midnight so." Naima shrugs then looks over at me.

"I want to party if y'all wanna—" Luna says, then mimes a joint with her fingers.

"We gotta wait til baseball season is over," Sam says.

"*He* gotta wait. I got you, baby girl." Darius winks at Luna, and she rolls her eyes. "You want in?" Darius asks me.

"Nah, man. I gotta take Naima home."

"Nigga, just spend the night. We staying at Sam's."

I mean I probably could spend the night. Amaya wouldn't

mind, and I don't even remember the last time I got high. I sigh then look at Naima. I gotta be responsible, though. This is prom, and I want her to have a good time, too.

"I'm good."

Darius shakes his head like he doesn't believe me. I half believe me too, but Sam changes the subject.

"So y'all coming to our last game next Thursday?"

"Of course." Naima wrinkles her nose. "You know how much I love baseball."

She hates all sports which she reminds me of every time I try to watch a NBA or NFL game with her.

"It's against Cherokee Central. We're gonna whoop their ass," Marcus chimes in.

"Haven't y'all lost most of your games this year?" Naima asks in her soft accent with the straightest face that makes it ten times funnier.

As I snort, Sam responds, "That's not important. We just gotta finish strong."

The guys high five each other and repeat, "Finish strong."

The rest of the food comes, and we eat. As soon as the music starts, Naima grabs Luna's hand and runs to the dance floor. While everyone else cares about how they dance and if they look cringe, Naima doesn't. She moves in whatever way she feels called which makes it more admirable. I grab my phone and record a few clips of her that I know she'll appreciate later and then sit back in my chair to check my email.

It's been a habit I've had almost every day for the past month. While Naima was applying to college, I sent my portfolio to galleries across the country and a few international ones as well. The deadline for a few of them passed a couple of months ago so I'm just waiting for an acceptance. So far, I've gotten one rejection, but there are still a dozen other places I'm waiting to hear from. The problem is I haven't told Naima any of this. She thinks I'm taking a gap year, and that's partially true. I'm not planning on going to college next year...or any year after that. The truth of that may devastate her as well as the truth of—

Naima grabs my shoulder, jolting me out of my thoughts. She's holding her hand out to me while the music slows down. I grab it and follow her to the dance floor. Laying her sweaty head on my shoulder, she presses her body into mine and sways. Damn, even her sweat smells good. I close my eyes, following along to her body and the music. Something hard and sharp slides between us, and when I open my eyes, Mrs. Berry, our calculus teacher, is there with a yardstick in her hand.

"Y'all need to keep Jesus between you," she says and presses the stick into my belly. I back away from Naima who I catch rolling her eyes.

"Sorry, Mrs. Berry." I smile knowing it'll diffuse the scowl on her face. It does, and she walks away. I cup Naima's jaw. She leans into it and hums. "Sorry about that," I say and bring her hand to my lips to kiss her knuckles. Softly. Apologetically.

"It's whatever." She tries to play it off but yawns. The fatigue sets in the corners of her face.

"You wanna sit down?" I ask.

"It's prom!" She releases herself from me and throws her hands in the air. "We're supposed to have fun."

"But we can take a break." I hold my hand out to give her the choice of taking it. Begrudgingly she does, so I lead her back to our seats. Her shoulder slumps, and her face softens when she looks back at the dance floor, at our friends dancing, talking, and laughing with each other.

"We can go home," I remind her. She has options other than exhausting herself to keep up with everybody else.

She rubs her eyes and then looks at me. "No, I'm fine. We can stay a bit longer." Naima squeezes my hand and offers a tired smile. She looks longingly at the dance floor for a few more songs until a pop song comes on. She instantly brightens and grabs me. "You have to dance with me."

I try to follow along with her dance moves. She twists and turns then punches the air and punches the dance floor. At one point she backs up on me and grinds, stopping when the chorus returns. Then, she jumps some more until the music finishes.

"Okay, I'm ready to go," she pants. "Let me go tell Luna."

Naima taps Luna's shoulder while she's dancing with some guy who's not her date.

"You're leaving? Noooo," Luna whines then hugs Naima. They squeeze each other for a good solid minute. "Ask your mom if I can spend the night. I'm not sleeping on Sam's couch."

"Okay, I will," Naima says. She looks around for Sam and then waves goodbye to him before we leave.

In the car, I ask her if she wants to get ice cream or something before I take her home. It's only 9:26.

"I just feel bad. This is your prom, and I'm making you leave early."

"You didn't make me do anything I didn't want to do," I reassure her.

Out of my peripheral, she stares at me then twists her lips. She's uncertain. I grab her hand and rub my thumb over her knuckles. "You don't have to go home yet. We can go somewhere else."

Her face brightens then. "Okay. Yes."

We drive to the nearest park and sit under the trees. Cracking the windows, I turn off the car, take off my suit jacket, get out of the driver's seat and into the backseat. Naima climbs over the seats to get into the back. She rests her head in my lap, and I rub her shoulders.

"Did you have fun at least?" I ask. The park light adds a soft warm light to the car, and the cicadas hum in the humid night air.

She sighs, "Why do people make such a big deal out of

prom? It's a lot of pressure to have a great time and to go all out. I mean it was fun, but it was no different than any other school dance."

"It's the last time we all get together and party before we graduate. That's a pretty big deal."

"I don't know. I guess the way people talked about it. I thought I'd feel differently."

"Yeah, I get that." Prom is more of an ideal than anything else. We think it's a bigger deal than it is because we've made it that way.

But I change the subject. Something I've learned that she likes is when I indulge her in her special interests and theories. It's always a fun thought experiment, and it's exciting to see where we end up.

"What's the latest theory?"

She hums, thinking about the question and then asks, "Are aliens racist?"

I choke-laugh. "Where did that come from?"

"I was watching a documentary about alien abductions and all the interviewees were white so either aliens are racist and only want white people or people of color don't talk about their alien abductions, but if aliens only want white people, why? Are aliens racist and hate the rest of us? Are they experimenting on white people? If so, why?"

That was a lot, but I ask, "Do you want to be abducted by aliens?"

"No!" she answers quickly. "That sounds terrifying. I just don't like the idea of aliens preferring white people. Like is white supremacy intergalactic?"

"If a species is advanced enough for intergalactic travel, I don't think they care about racial politics. Maybe Black folks just don't talk about alien abductions cause they'll probably lock us up."

"That could be it, but I don't know," she yawns. "It doesn't sit right with me that aliens are racist."

I rub her shoulder while she stammers through a sentence, "I just—it doesn't." After a few seconds she gives up and breathes softly. Her eyelids flutter shut, and she's out. I rub her arm a little bit longer. She looks so peaceful, and it's going to be my fault when she's not anymore. I sigh knowing that in one-hundred and five days, I'm going to break her heart.

CHAPTER THREE

Naima

I slide the pencil against the back of Kamron's ear. He twitches, and I have to bite my lip down to suppress the grin. Mrs. Evans, our AP English Literature teacher, is going on and on about Zora Neale Hurston and her role in the Harlem Renaissance. Why Mrs. Evans waits until we have two days left of school is beyond me. We've taken our AP Exams. We've declared which colleges we're going to. We've already had prom. Now it's just graduation next week and then we're done with high school. Why is she prolonging this?

Kamron reaches behind him grabbing my knee to get me to stop. I do but not before letting a giggle escape. Mrs. Evans stops briefly to glance at me before she returns to the Google Slides. I roll my eyes when she does.

Kamron and I take most of our classes together this year, and he's been such a balm in all of them. When I get anxious and need to stim, he lets me use him to stim. When it's a class where we sit next to each other, I can fidget with his hand under the desk. In English, there's only six of us, and we all have to sit in the front. I sit right behind him, and it gives me the perfect view of his darling head. He's been growing his hair out, and it's beautiful and thick on the top and tapered on the sides, but I love when he lets Amaya do fun things with it. Like right now, he's still wearing his prom hairstyle. It's small cornrows in the middle feeding into chunky cornrows down the side of his head and then a smaller cornrow on the outside of the chunky ones. All of that ties into a small bun. I reach up and dangle his bun. I want to give him a kiss right in the middle part of his head. I chew my bottom lip and bounce my knee to suppress the urge, but now that I've started thinking about it, that's all I can think about.

Kamron grabs my hand and squeezes it. The touch gets me out of my head and calms me. I twirl his fingers around mine and use that to focus on the rest of Mrs. Evans' lecture. She's assigning *Their Eyes Were Watching God* and having us discuss it on the last day of school for a participation grade. My God, when does it end?

As she's passing out the books, the bell saves us from any more unnecessary assignments so we can go to lunch. The last week of school is when the cafeteria decides it wants to start experimenting with lunch. Instead of the usual calendar that tells me whether or not I need to bring lunch, every day is TBD so I bring my own. Luna is already in the cafeteria sitting at our usual table. Kamron braves the lunch line. I plop the assigned book down with my lunch bag.

"Are you getting new assignments this week too?" I ask her as I sit down.

"No, who would assign something this close to graduation?" Luna asks because she's a reasonable human being unlike Mrs. Fucking Evans.

I emote wide eyes and bob my head like *Exactly!* By the time Kamron sits down, I'm still ranting about the new assignment and wondering how much it'd ruin my A if I didn't do it. When he joins us, it's just the three of us to make our table complete. This year Sam has second lunch so besides us driving to school in the mornings together, I barely see him. He's usually with his "partner" Dixie after school. That's what they call each other because apparently boyfriend/girlfriend is old-fashioned or something. I don't know. But I spend my lunches with my bestie Luna and my *boyfriend* Kamron. It'd be nice to see Sam more though. I guess that's what the baseball game is for in a few days.

"It's a Black classic, and it's pretty good. I think you'd like it," Kamron says.

"Of course you've already read it." I throw my hands in the air. If it has anything to do with Black literature, he knows it all. I'm not saying I don't read Black literature. I've had to read some for AP Lit, but I'm more of a contemporary fantasy kind of girl. I'm here for Tracy Deonn and Namina Forna, not so much for Toni Morrison and James Baldwin.

He interlocks his fingers with mine and squeezes. "We can read it today after school," he offers.

"Are you staying for dinner?" I ask.

"I can."

"And where's my invite?" Luna asks.

"I can come over this weekend or you can come to mines?" When I think about it, her house has Nellie, her black cat, and Mexican and Puerto Rican food. "Nevermind, I'll go to your house."

After dinner, Kamron sits with me in my room while I'm struggling to read *Their Eyes Were Watching God*. He's not rereading it because he claims he remembers most of it. I keep shifting with the book trying to replace "lak" with "like." Every other word is "de" instead of "the." It's so annoying, and it's slowing me down. I don't know how I'm gonna finish it by Thursday.

"Don't you think it's weird that Mrs. Evans gave us another book to read?" I vent to avoid reading the book. "We literally could've done nothing this week like the rest of our classes. The AP Exams were last week!"

"She could've," he says, "But this was the first time she assigned us a Black novel to read all year."

That's not right because I read Toni Morrison and Richard Wright this year.

"You read those books on your own," Kamron says, reading my mind. "Even *Othello*, which is written by Shakespeare, She told us to read over Christmas break, and when we got back, she said it didn't matter. Probably just because it was written about a Black man."

"Dang, have we ever been assigned any books by people of color?" I ask.

We got to read a novel of our choosing each quarter, and I chose books by people of color, but when I think about it, Mrs. Evans never assigned any to us. I fell in love with Kate Chopin, Edgar Allen Poe, and William Faulkner's stories. I had to stomach Eudora Welty and John Steinback, but in my free time I read Toni Morrison and James Baldwin and Richard Wright. I wasn't always a fan of their writing, but it was the first time I read a book for class with Black characters.

"For as long as I've been in Mississippi, no," Kamron answers. "This is our first."

I try to remember my assigned reading over the years. My English class never read books or stories by people of color which is a shame considering that half of our school is Black. I used to think that we weren't as bad as other schools, especially those in Florida, because we didn't have book bans, but the teachers just never bothered to assign us any of those books.

"It's kinda racist when you think about it," Kamron continues. "A third of our English class is Black, and we have to read their stories, but they never have to read ours."

The third is me and him. There are only six people in our AP Lit class.

I stare at him. What does it mean for me who has never read that deep into what was going on around me? I was so busy trying to do my work well, I never even questioned what the work was or how it was impacting me. What does that say about me?

"You're right," I tell him. "I can't believe I never saw it before."

"Most of the teachers here are covertly racist. If you blink, you miss it," he says.

"But they've all been nice to you." When it was just me in the advanced class, it was easy for me to say they were racist, but when Kamron came along and the teachers were nice to him, but mean to me, I figured it was more ableism than racism.

"Yeah, cause I'm one of the 'good ones,'" he finger quotes. "Earlier this year Mrs. Evans claimed my paper was AI because it was too 'well-written,' and don't get me started on Mrs. Truss."

Mrs. Truss was our AP Biology teacher who hated me and knew that I didn't get along with Kamron when he first came here. She assigned us to be lab partners which worked out well for us, so maybe I should thank her for helping me get a boyfriend.

"Yeah. Incredibly ableist."

"And racist. Why she pit the only two Black people against

each other?"

"She didn't really pit us against each other," I argue.

"She was constantly playing mind games trying to make it seem like you were bad for speaking your mind. Like Black people are only good when we're obedient."

"You were obedient?"

"I was *respectful,* but I saw how she treated you. That's why I kept trying to speak up for you in class."

"You did?"

"Are you oblivious to everything?"

Instead of malice in his voice, there's a soft amazement. He cups my cheek and caresses my jaw with his thumb. He stares at me softly to the point where my heart flutters. My breath deepens.

"You really shouldn't look at me like that," I whisper. Mom is literally downstairs.

"Like what?" His lips quirks in amusement.

He's such a tease!

"Shut up!" I playfully push his shoulder but then I grab his face. "Actually, I just wanna—"

I bring his face closer to mine until his lips are just a taste away and wait. He reaches his arm around my waist and closes the kiss. His bow shaped lips are pillowy soft and perfectly press into mine. When he pulls away, I bring his lips back to mine. It's like as soon as the kiss is over, I have amnesia and need another one ASAP. I kiss him again and again.

"You have to stop," I groan. "I gotta read this book."

"*I* have to stop?"

"Yes, you gotta stop looking like that so I can do my homework. You're such a distraction."

When he grins, I just want to press my body against his and kiss him again.

"Ughh, you're the worst. I have to read this difficult ass book. Stop it."

"Let me read it to you," he offers. I hesitate because I hate when people read to me, but maybe with him, it's different. "It's better when you listen to it anyway. You can hear the rhythms of the words."

"Fine," I slide down on the bed and lay on him. He wraps his arm around me, and I bury my face in the woodsy scent of his warm chest.

"Where are you in the book?"

"You can start at the beginning."

And he does. His voice is strong as he reads, its usual staccato slipping as he softens the endings of his words, making them smooth and dark like molasses. He sounds Southern, country, and Black. I close my eyes and listen to his heartbeat's lullaby as his voice lulls me to sleep.

CHAPTER FOUR

Kamron

Naima, Luna, and I walk down the bleachers to the front row of the baseball field. We're behind the dugout giving us a good view of home plate. Pulling the plastic seats down to sit, they're scolding hot. Everything is hot, and the muggy air doesn't make it any better. I bring my water bottle to my lips and sip, tug my baseball cap on my head. It's been so long since I've gotten to sit and watch a baseball game. Pops used to have season passes for the San Francisco Giants and pre-pandemic, we'd go at least once a week.

I sigh. Pre-pandemic life.

Naima places her hand on my arm.

"Hmm," I turn to her.

"We're gonna get some snacks. You want anything?"

"Nah, I'm good." I smile at her.

Her and Luna walk back up the steps to the concession stand. Looking around at the bleachers, it's mostly empty. It's expected with the team's losing streak, but I thought with it being the last game, more people would show up and support. Guess I was wrong.

The players are in the outfield stretching and warming up. I stand up to join them, whirling my arms around, stretching my neck and shoulders before sitting down again, waiting for the game to start. I can't believe school is over. Today was our last day. There's still graduation next week which feels like a formality at this point, but I never thought I'd get this far. I never thought I'd be here.

After graduation we have the whole summer ahead of us and then after that? I close my eyes and breathe. I have to break up with the love of my life, and she'll hate me for it. I haven't told her yet because I'm holding onto hope that something will change, just long enough for me to figure out how to create a life for me and Naima when she goes to college, but right now I have nothing.

I lean back in the seat right as Luna and Naima return.

"We got cheese fries and gummies and more water. Also do you need sunscreen? We just sprayed down." Naima asks.

Now that she's mentioned it, my neck feels like it's burning. I nod, and she hands the snacks to Luna, puts the waters down, and slides her backpack to one side.

"You want spray or lotion. It's white lotion so you'll be white, but you won't burn."

"I'll take the lotion," I say.

She squirts some in her palm and smears it. "Where do you want it?"

"Just on my neck and shoulder." I turn my back to make it easier for her, and she slides into the seat behind me. Rubbing the lotion on my neck, I close my eyes to savor this touch, this bit of closeness while I still have it. While I still have her. She's so careful to not get any on my hair or shirt, but I don't even care about that. I only care about her.

"I rubbed it in as best I could," she says, wiping the residue on her own thighs.

"Thanks," I kiss her cheek, smelling the sweat and sunscreen on her skin.

She smiles at me, and I want her to look at me like that forever.

The game finally starts, and the leadoff hitter hits a homerun from the first pitch. I knew our team stunk but this? I suck in a breath.

"Is that bad?" Naima asks.

"They just hit a home run."

"That's good, right?" She claps her hands.

"It's the opposing team."

"Oh."

I point to Marcus playing shortstop. "You see Marcus and Darius and Sam?" I point to them in center and right field. "They're all on the field playing defense. Their job is to make sure the other team doesn't score runs. When they're batting, their job is to get a run. A home run then is good."

"I actually got that, I think," she says. "You're so much better at explaining this than Sam. He just yells and then he's like, 'Why don't you get it?'" She waves her hands in the air frustrated, imitating Sam.

Maybe that's what I can do this summer. Show her stuff so that when I'm gone, she'll always remember me.

It's the bottom of the first, and the home team is batting. When the ball goes out of the zone, the batter doesn't swing.

"Good eye!" I yell and clap.

"What does that mean?" Naima asks.

"Every time he swings, it's a strike," I explain. "If the pitcher throws it in the zone, and he doesn't swing, it's a strike, but if the pitcher throws it out of the zone, it's a ball, and when you get four balls, you walk."

"Okay," she nods. "I think I got that."

"How do you know so much about baseball?" Luna asks.

"I used to play Little League."

Naima gasps. "You never told me."

"Yeah, it was back before the pandemic. I used to play first." I point to first base, and they both turn to look at it.

"Did you like it?" Luna asks.

"I loved it." The excitement from Saturday morning games. Hitting the ball as hard as I could and watching it fly out. Catching the other team's pop up balls. Being friends with my teammates and trying to one up each other. The rush from sliding into home plate. Practicing with Pops during off season. What isn't there to love?

"Then why'd you stop?" Naima asks me. Her doe-eyes wide with anticipation of an answer I don't want to give. Why would I quit something I love? It seems like the universe keeps setting my life up that way.

"The pandemic," I answer, mostly truthfully. "Never picked it up again."

She studies my face somberly. Probably noticing the sadness in my voice. I smile to throw her off. "But you know what? I don't have to play baseball to love it."

She smiles again. Whew.

"Who's your favorite baseball player?" she asks.

"Shohei Ohtani," I answer easily. "His stats are incredible. Some people say he's better than Babe Ruth, but you can't really compare them because that was a different time. When he was still an Angel, Pops and I got to see him play. Top five baseball experiences."

Naima scrolls on her phone and then faces it to me showing me images of Shohei. "This him?"

"Yeah"

She hums, thoughtfully scrolling through images of Shohei. "Yeah, he looks like a pretty, um, good baseball player."

She slides her phone into her pocket then says, "We should watch the game."

Luna shakes her head when Naima leans back in the seat and

crosses her arms.

The next five innings are scoreless. There are times when batters get on base, but no one's scored a run. For the seventh inning stretch, we stand and Naima looks toward the entrance.

"I can't believe she didn't come," she says, directed more towards Luna than me.

"Who?" I ask.

"Dixie," she says, turning to give Luna a look. She sighs then places her hand on my arm. "We're gonna go to the bathroom, okay?"

I nod, watching them ascend the steps. They don't return until the eighth inning, and the score's still 1-0. At least the team's good at defense.

In the ninth inning, Darius hits first. He strikes out looking. Next is Sam who watches the pitches but doesn't swing.

"Good eye!" Naima yells.

"That was a strike," I whisper in her ear.

"Strikes are bad?" Her nose wrinkles.

"Yeah."

Sam ends up drawing a walk and jogs to first base. The next batter hits a pop up ball that's caught easily. It's two outs. One more out, and our team loses.

Marcus comes up to hit. The first three pitches are balls then he takes the pitch for 3-1. On the next pitch, Marcus swings and the ball goes up and out to left center field. I expect it to drop, but it keeps going until it lands over the gate.

"Oh, they got a home-run," Naima says nonchalantly.

"We won!" I yell and pump my fist in the air

"We won? Oh my god. They won!"

She stands beside me to celebrate. Sam and Marcus jog over the bases, and as Sam steps on home plate, he looks to Naima who's smiling and waving at him. Something about the way he smiles back at her makes me uneasy.

Chapter Five

Naima

The senior baseball players are all meeting up at Sam's to celebrate the win and the end of the school year. As soon as we came home from the game, I washed the thick layer of sweat and sunscreen off my skin and took a nap. Now I'm in my pajamas sitting on Sam's porch watching the group of boys loudly celebrate around the bonfire they built. Kamron's laughing and celebrating with them. I think it's kinda cute how he said "*We* won" like he was on the field with them and not watching it with us.

I pull my legs into my chest and lay my head on my knee. This is really it. I've been waiting for the end of school for as long as I can remember. In the fall, I'll be attending Millsaps College and majoring in biochemistry. That's been my dream for years, and I'm so excited that I get to start over and don't have to be the weird autistic girl whose father died. I'll get to be me without all the assumptions and labels.

Fun fact: The first diagnosed autistic person, Donald Triplett, was born in Mississippi and attended Millsaps College so maybe I'll be around more open-minded people. Maybe they'll be more accepting of who I am. But I'll have to face those maybes without Luna and Sam. They're moving on just like I am.

The door opens, and Luna emerges with a hard seltzer in her hand.

"Girl, quit sitting here being depressed and come on." She tugs my arm, leading me to the bonfire. Kamron's face lights up when he sees me, and he puts his arm around me. I lay on his shoulder. Although I won't have my friends next year, at least I'll have Kamron. He's taking a gap year until he decides where he wants to go to college.

He plants a kiss on the top of my head. "You doing okay, baby?" he asks.

The way Kamron calls me baby, it reverberates throughout my body and travels to my hands and toes. I muster a smile for him and nod. He kisses my temple this time before saying, "Alright, I'mma holla at Darius real quick. Be right back."

He dabs up Darius. They walk closer to the wall of trees bordering Sam's yard and light up a joint. Kamron smokes? I don't know why it's shocking. I'm probably the only teenager who hasn't smoked or drank, but I just thought he was different. I thought he was more like me.

"You okay?" Sam asks, his drawl thicker from beer. He rubs

my back, and I lay my head on his chest, smelling the shower and fabric softener on his T-shirt.

"Why does everybody keep asking me that?"

"You have this blank look on your face. I was just checking." He sips his beer and studies me.

"I'm fine. I just—" I sigh.

"Talk to me." He rubs my arm.

Although the touch softens the waves of turmoil swirling in me, Luna's right. This isn't a time to be sitting around being depressed. It's a time to celebrate.

"You won your game. We should be talking about you. Congratulations. I guess you were right, and I was wrong."

"I'm always right." He grins, digging in his pocket for his phone. "Can you say that again so I can record it?"

I roll my eyes while he chuckles.

He takes another sip of his beer before asking. "You ready to get your license yet?"

Junior year Sam started teaching me how to drive. We got into a very scary altercation with a deer and had to postpone lessons for a while, but by the end of last summer, I stopped death-gripping the wheel, and now I feel pretty okay driving. I rigidly adhere to the speed limit and am still super vigilant of deer, but I'm much better than when I started. Not confident or great, but okay.

"Do you think I'm ready?" I look up at him. To be honest, I love our driving lessons. It's one of the few chances I get to spend time with him, and I don't want that to come to an end.

"I wouldn't let you drive me around if I didn't think so," he says.

When I first dated Kamron, he wanted to pick me up in the mornings and take me to school instead of me riding with Sam. Besides being a major waste of time (Sam lives right next to me; Kamron lives fifteen minutes away), Kamron's a really aggressive driver. He slams on the brake, and it took two weeks of motion sickness before I decided Sam could take me to school in the morning, and Kamron could drop me off in the afternoon. Sometimes Sam would let me drive us to school in the mornings. He'd still be holding onto the grab bar on his side when I drove.

But maybe he's right though, and I'm finally ready. "How about we go after graduation?"

He sips his beer and nods. Right then, a black Camry pulls into the driveway. It's Dixie's car. So she couldn't show up to his game, but she shows up to the after party?

"Gotta go." He slides his arm from around me and starts walking backwards. "Thanks for coming to my game. I'm glad you were there." He turns and walks towards Dixie. As they hug, she looks up at him to talk to him about something. Probably some sorry excuse for missing his game. Has she been to any games this season?

My jaw clenches so I direct my attention to the flame instead, feeling the heat of the dancing yellows and oranges and reds. Kamron and Darius walk back to the bonfire, and Darius dabs him up before leaving.

"You looked like you were having fun," I say.

"Yeah, we talked." Kamron says. In the firelight, I can see the white of his eyes have turned a yellow reddish color.

"I didn't know you smoked."

He scratches his neck. "Yeah. I used to back in the day. It's been a while."

How long of a while? He hasn't smoked in the almost two years we've been together. Instead of asking more questions, I drop it. I've learned two new things about Kamron today, and although I love learning more about him, this feels more like a secret. I mean Sam and Luna have been participating in their "recreational activities" for years, but I didn't know this about Kamron. I wonder what other secrets he's hiding from me.

He grabs my hand and leads me to the porch where he sits against the wall. I sit across from him hesitantly, not knowing how he is under the influence. He's smiling. His head leans back against the wall before rolling around to face me. He reaches his hands out for mine. I slowly place them on his, and he yanks me towards him.

"Sorry," he apologizes. His finger traces my face searching for some injury. "You okay?"

I nod. He smiles, a little weaker than usual, but still as beautiful. Relief relaxes my tightened chest. I smile back at him. He brings one of my hands up to his lips and kisses my knuckles.

"You are the best thing that ever happened to me. You know that?"

My heart flutters in response to the sincerity in his voice. He loves me. Why am I freaking out about him smoking weed?

"I love you," I say.

He wraps his arms around my waist and stares at my lips. The smoky peppery scent wafts off his tongue and into my mouth as he kisses me. With both hands, I grasp his face and press my body into his, kissing him harder. He moans, but it dies in the back of his throat. I hum in response, wanting more of his guttural sounds, when he pulls away for air.

Panting, his finger gently tugs my bottom lip when he says, "I love you, too, baby."

Chapter Six

Naima

It's just my luck that I have to walk behind and sit beside my cousin, Kennedy, who absolutely hates me. She's beloved by pretty much everyone, as evidenced by her being crowned prom queen. We used to be best friends when we were little, but after I was diagnosed with autism, she—along with a good chunk of our family—abandoned me. After Kamron moved to Mississippi, she wanted to date him, but he chose me, so now she *really* hates me.

The first graduation practice, I tried to be cordial. She wore a highlighted curly lob wig, and I told her it was cute. The next day, she installed a whole new wig.

When graduation comes, all the girls stand in a room off to the side of the coliseum waiting for it to start. I'm dressed in my maroon gown, white cap, and gold honors stole. The school colors. Mom, Markese, and my cousin Eric are here. Eric's staying with us this summer, he didn't say why, but Mom is always excited to have family come around. She's told me that she doesn't blame me for them abandoning us, but it doesn't stop me from feeling guilty that they cut her off too.

Principal Lewis enters the room and tells us to line up because the ceremony is about to start. We do as he says, walking single file onto the stage while the audience claps. Someone from the administration opens the graduation with a prayer and then the valedictorian and salutatorian give their speeches. It's mostly about overcoming and moving on to the next stage of our lives. I struggle to not roll my eyes knowing that those two have never struggled a day in their lives.

Thankfully their boring speeches end, and the front row lines up to start receiving their diplomas. We're segregated. Girls are in alphabetical order and then boys are behind us. I don't know why they thought we couldn't sit next to each other for an hour. Do adults really have so little faith in us?

Once we get to my row, my heartbeat drums in my ears. Luna is one of the first ones to walk across the stage. She smiles, and her family whoops in the background. I smile cause I know the whistle is from her dad, Mr. Hernandez. A few more people walk and then Kennedy—the audience erupts when she walks across. She waves to the audience and then shakes Principal Lewis's hands. Everybody's so happy that she exists.

And then it's me. It's like day and night. There's a delayed whoop from one person, probably Eric, which makes it worse than the silence. Once I get to Principal Lewis's hands, he hands me the diploma and smooshes his lips together in that uncomfortable white people's smile, "Congratulations, Naima."

"Thank you," I smirk.

All four years of high school, I have been in and out of his office. I'm an exceptional student when it comes to grades. A bit of nuisance when it comes to the social aspects of school and the unspoken rules of a "well-behaved" student. I used to be in his office at least once a month, but when I started dating Kamron, I don't know, something about having him there in my classes settled me. Whenever I was confused or frustrated or upset, I would write a note to him, and he'd write helping me to process what was going on. Don't get me wrong, I've still been sent to the principal's office this year, but it's been like three times instead of twelve.

I grab my diploma with glee and return to my seat. Thirteen years are in my hand. K-12. I made it. I actually made it.

When Kamron walks across the stage, I cheer from my seat. A few of the administrators turn their head because it's in poor taste apparently. There's another girl who cheers from the audience. It must be his sister. His family is in town. I've met his aunt who he lives with and his grandparents who live in the Delta, but I've yet to meet his parents and sister. He talks so much about them, but I'll finally get to meet them this weekend which is nerve-wracking.

Sam is the last of our friend group to walk across the stage.

His fans cheer for him. I wonder if Dixie actually cared enough to show up.

Once all the names have been called, Principal Lewis says a few words of farewell and then signals for us to throw our caps in the air. We do, and when I catch mine, I'm surrounded by smiling faces. Luna rushes over to squeeze me.

"We did it!" she says, and we hug each other while moving in a circle.

Then Kamron pops up and joins our group hug. "I gotta go see my family," he says. "But I'll see you tomorrow, right?"

I nod and watch him walk into the crowd. Luna also leaves to find her family and Ricky who made a surprise appearance. I look towards the back of the stage where Sam is surrounded by a bunch of boys.

"Hey," I wrap my arms around him, and he completes the hug.

"We graduated. Let's go!" he yells, and when I jump, he rubs my back. "Oh sorry. Hey, we're gonna go to Marcus's after this. You wanna come?"

"Nope, I'm good," I say, releasing my arms from around him. "Y'all have fun though. I'm gonna find Mom."

He nods as I walk off stage and push through the crowd. Mom spots me first and yells my name. When I reach her, she squeezes me. "I'm so proud of you, Naima."

"Thanks, Mom."

When she finally releases me, tears pool up in her eyes.

"You're just getting so grown. It felt like yesterday that we brought you home and—"

"Mom!" I throw my head back, exasperated.

She waves her hand in front of her face trying to slow her tears.

"You're a woman now."

"Auntie, can we go?" Eric loops his arm around Mom's. "Congrats, Cuz."

"Where's Markese?" I scan the room and see him near the exit talking to a friend.

"You ain't going to a party or nothing?" Eric asks.

I shake my head. "I just wanna go home. I'm tired."

I'm more than tired. My brain is buzzing, but my body feels so heavy. I want to lay in bed and not get up for at least two weeks, but tomorrow I'm meeting Kamron's parents, and I have to be well-rested to make the best impression possible. I really hope they like me.

Chapter Seven

Kamron

"I already don't like this girl," Mama says, and it's devastating. She hasn't even given Naima a chance. If she just met her and talked to her, she'd see how brilliant and wonderful she is.

"You said you were coming here for a year. *One year.* To 'get a fresh start,'" she says with air quotes. "We say, 'Okay.' A year passes and then you say, 'Let me graduate in Mississippi.' We let you and now it's 'Just for the summer.' All for *some girl,*" she says the last part with a nasty bite in her voice.

"Naima's not just some girl. I need a little more time." I close my eyes and pinch the bridge of my nose. How many times do I have to have this conversation with her?

"And then what? You're gonna call us to say you're staying *another* year," she shakes her head. "No, we're cutting you off."

"Mama, no! I'm coming home."

"Liyah," Pops swoops in. "He's coming home." He mouths

I got this to me and then talks to Mama.

I leave her to go back to my room and plop on the bed. It's 11:15, and under two hours until the party starts. Mama says it's for me, but mostly it's to see our "country cousins" that she hasn't seen since she was a child and used to visit Mississippi every summer.

Amaya knocks on my door, and I sit up.

"Sorry about your ma."

"She was your sister first."

She makes a face as if she's sorry about that too and sits beside me on the bed.

"Listen, I love having you here, Nephew. You can stay for as long as you like, but she misses you. She's shit at showing it, but—"

"I know," I sigh. I'm not gonna lie, it's been nice to be away from the watchful eye of my mother these past two years. I can go wherever I want, do whatever I want, and be whoever I want without any input from her, but now that's over with. All the freedom Amaya's given me will be gone when I move back to California.

I lay down on the bed, and Amaya places her hand on my knee. "Go pick up Naima. We'll work on your ma until she gets here."

I grab my keys and slip out the garage door to avoid Mama. Once inside, I exhale a long deep breath. Hopefully Amaya's right, and she can calm Mama down. Knowing Mama though, she'll be so busy putting on a show for our family that she'll forget I'm there. I can bring Naima here, show her off, and leave with as little harm to her as possible. Let's hope.

I text Naima I'm on my way, start the car, and drive to her house. When I get there, she's already on the porch smiling and waving at me. She's wearing a sundress, Crocs, and a bandana tied in the front. All in various shades of green. She looks adorable, but then I think about Mama. What would she say if she saw Naima? Her greens don't match? Did a child pick out her outfit for her? She looks like a country bumpkin? Maybe this was a mistake. Maybe I shouldn't have tried to blend my two worlds together. My life with Naima is perfect and better untouched from the rest of my family.

Naima slides into the passenger seat and kisses my cheek. I grab her hand and interlock our fingers. She's here with me. She's mine. I just have to stay calm.

"How was your night?" I ask, trying to get my mind off the mess at Amaya's.

"I cried," she says, her face expressionless. Yep. This is the worst idea.

"What's wrong?"

"I don't know," she shakes her head. "I just been feeling really down lately. Like we're *high school graduates*, and I expected to be happy, but I've been sad about it for some reason."

I bet the "some reason" is Luna moving to Mexico, Sam and Dixie moving to LA, and me going back to Sacramento, even if she doesn't know that part yet. I swallow the lump in my throat.

"I'm sure it's a normal feeling. Change is ambivalent, you know?"

I remember when I was learning more about autism. Naima's a Level 1 Autistic so transitions, among other things that we don't even think about, stresses her out and causes a full-body response in her. Going from high school to college can be stressful for anyone, but it's more challenging for her.

"Yeah," she sighs and leans back against the seat. "Maybe that's it."

I back out of the driveway and head back to my house. Naima is near silent, and I have no idea what's going through her head because she doesn't involuntarily wear her emotions on her face like the rest of us. I just hope everyone's nice to her when we get there.

Cars have already filled our driveway so I have to park on the street. I help Naima out of the car, and we walk towards the front door that's covered in balloons. Blues music plays from the backyard. Before we get to the door, my older cousin Anthony turns the corner of the house.

"Cuz, is that you?" he asks, holding a brown paper sack in his hands. He has on a Pirates baseball cap, a plain tee, basketball shorts, and Nikes.

I dap him up and deepen my voice to answer him. "Yeah. How you doing?"

"Damn, you getting grown on me. I remember you used to be this tall—" he lowers his palm to his mid-thigh—"running around here. Now you 'bout grown."

What he talking about 'bout grown'? I *am* grown. Or at least I'll be when I turn eighteen in a few weeks, but that don't mean that I'm not already a man.

Anthony turns his attention to Naima. "And who's this little lady?"

"I'm Naima." She waves.

He turns towards me with mischievous eyes. "Awww, I see you, Cuz. Nice to meet you Miss Naima." He shakes her hand before patting me on the shoulder and walking away.

Anthony. I exhale and squeeze her fingers trying to calm us both down. One family member down. A bunch more to go.

When I open the door, everyone turns towards us.

"Hey y'all, what's good?" I smile, wrapping my arm around Naima's waist.

A few relatives pat me on the back and congratulate me before Mama walks up to us with a glass of wine in her hand. She hugs Naima telling her it's good to meet her. I don't know who this woman is that's replacing Mama, but I'll take her any day.

Mama says, "Kamron's told me so much about you. You're an honor student, right? And you're going to Millsaps in the fall?

"Yes, I'm majoring in Biochemistry," she chirps.

"That's...ambitious," Mama nods then looks at me. "If you'll excuse me, I have to go find your father."

We watch her leave and then Naima whispers, "Did I do okay?"

"You were fine," I reassure her. Mama was...weird. When Naima coughs, I rub her shoulder. "Is everything alright?"

"Her perfume was really strong," she whispers, then presses her palm against her nose.

"We can go outside if you—"

"No, I'm fine. I'll be okay," she tries to reassure me. Just like at prom, she tries to power through things to not be a nuisance to anyone else.

"Well *I* would like to go outside if you wanna join me."

She giggles seeing right through me. "Fine."

She takes my hand while I lead her to the back door hoping to sit down somewhere, but Nana's there.

"Congratulations, baby!" She hugs me.

"Thanks Nana." Tears glaze her blue eyes.

"Oh and congrats, Naima." She gives her an equally tight hug. "I heard you were showing out this year."

"Yeah I know. I beat Kamron." She grins.

"Class rank means nothing now that we graduated." She was third in our class. I was seventh.

"That's what losers say." She sticks her tongue out at me.

"Well I'm gonna get out of this sun and let you two argue," Nana says, wiping the sweat from her brow. "Naima, let me know if you're growing watermelons this year. I'd love to pay you for one."

Naima's smile dampens, and she bites her lower lip. "I'm not gardening this year cause it won't be ready 'til after I'm at college."

When Naima mentions college, Nana looks at me. She wants me to tell her, and I will, but it's also the first year that she hasn't gardened since her dad died. I don't want to add onto what she's already going through.

Nana places a hand on Naima's shoulder and says, "That's alright, baby. I'm so proud of you for getting into Millsaps. It's a great school." Nana places her other hand on my shoulder and says, "I'm proud of you both, even if Naima beat you."

Naima giggles as Nana walks between us and back into the house. She seems happier and comfortable now which is what I wanted and what she needed.

"You feeling better?"

"What?" she asks.

She forgot. Of course.

"Your—" I wave my fingers near my nose.

"Oh, yeah." She nods. "Much better. Thank you."

Back when we first met, I was trying to impress her, and I may have overdone it with the cologne. Okay, I definitely overdid it, but I was listening to some guy on TikTok about how to get a girl's attention, and I got her attention. Just not in a good way, you know? She got a migraine because I tripped off her senses, and I felt real guilty about that, but now I know better.

She wraps her arm around my waist, lays her head on my shoulder, and exhales a deep breath. I hold her and lay my head gently against hers. She always smells sweet, like she was spawned in a bakery or something.

"Can I meet your sister?" She lifts her head to ask me.

"Yeah, she's around here somewhere." Jada was asleep when I left this morning, but when I open the door, she's sitting on the couch fooling around with the playlist. She looks up right as we walk over to her, gets up from the couch, and hugs Naima.

"It's so good to finally meet you. I can't believe Kamron waited so long to introduce us."

"Yeah, me too," Naima agrees.

Jada's three years older than me. She's an African-American studies major at UCLA.

We all sit on the couch together. Jada crosses her legs and faces Naima, "I have to ask. Are you Muslim?"

A puzzled look crosses Naima's face. "Um...no."

"Your name. It's Arabic so I just—"

"Oh, yeah. I am named after a Black Muslim lady. She went to college with my dad. He claimed she was a friend, but I think that's just the story he told Mom so they could name me after her. He said that it was the most beautiful name he ever heard."

Jada's face is so full of sympathy I want to knock it off her.

I told them her dad died, but she doesn't have to treat Naima like a wounded puppy. If anything she loves talking about her dad and the memory of him. It makes me wish I could've met him. He seemed like he was a cool guy so I shake my head at Jada to cut it.

"I love your hair," Naima says. Jada's braids are in a bun on the top of her head.

"I can do yours while I'm here if you like," Jada offers.

"Really?" Naima smiles.

She wants to get Naima alone for hours and talk to her. About what? Is she gonna tell Naima I'm leaving before I get to?

"Are you sure you wanna do that? It's gonna take forever," I say to deter the worst case scenario from happening.

Jada smiles. My sinister sister. "I have all the time in the world. Why don't you let us girls talk, okay?"

I unclench my jaw and breathe. Turning to Naima, I ask, "You gonna be okay?"

She places her hand on my thigh. "I'll be fine."

There's a moment where we study the other to silently check in. She doesn't emote any hesitation so I take another look at Jada before getting up and joining Mama and Pops talking in the kitchen.

"How much did you tell her?" Mama whispers when I reach her.

"I told her I was taking a gap year. She thinks I'm staying

with Amaya," I sigh gazing back at her sitting on the couch with Jada. She deserves the truth, but I'm too afraid to tell her, too afraid to end our relationship.

"So she knows nothing?" Mama asks at the same time Pops asks, "When are you gonna tell her?"

My jaw clenches. There's a lot going on at once, and I really don't want to answer either question. Pops places his hand on my shoulder and squeezes.

"Go. Calm down in your room."

I exhale then nod before heading to my studio instead. The bumping music bounces off the wall and the smell of damp clay meeting my nose when I sit down at my wheel instantly calms me. Reaching over to my work table, I grab a wheel bat and a ball of wedged clay. I wet the bat before slamming the clay on it to start centering it. I breathe in when I cone up, breathe out when I cone down. Once the clay is centered, I create a divet with my fingers to open the clay up. My entire focus shifts to pulling my walls, making sure they're nice and even so by the time I've created a cylinder, I'm breathing much easier. Grabbing the cylinder, I play with the form of the clay until it break. Then I scrape it off, form a ball to reuse, and clean up.

Settling into my studio's armchair, I realize I have ninety days until Naima starts college. Ninety days to tell her the truth—that I'm moving to California, and there's a good chance I won't ever be back. Ninety days to end our relationship.

But I also have ninety days left with her so I should focus on that instead of sitting and wallowing in here.

I walk out of my studio and return to Naima and Jada talking on the couch.

Jada looks up at me, "Don't you think Naima just looks like an artist? She has this eclectic look about her."

"I told her I don't have a creative bone in my body," Naima giggles while filling me in on their conversation.

I smile at how easily she's slipping into my family, how animated and comfortable she is with Jada. I don't care what my parents say. I'm gonna find a way to be with her. I want to marry her. Marriage? I don't know why I never thought of it, but that's the perfect idea: Naima as my wife. That's my end goal. I know she doesn't like to rush things, but I can't help but get hyped about it. Naima could be my wife someday.

A hand rests on my thigh. "Why you smiling?" Naima asks, her doe-eyes wide. A slight smile tugs on her lips.

I wrap my arm further around her shoulder and kiss her cheek, "Because I love you that's why."

And I can't wait to make you a permanent part of my family.

Chapter Eight

Naima

I run my hands over my Fulani braids. The style is old, but I've always wanted to try it, and I can't cornrow. Jada did such a good job. She made a custom blonde blend for me, and she's so cool. She dresses like boho chic—all long skirts and crop tops and head scarfs or wraps. I wish I had some sort of style like that. Instead—I look down at my crop top and overalls—I dress like a toddler.

Their family is so cool and creative and smart. Jada majors in African-American studies, and she knows so much about Black history and Black philosophy and I don't know. It makes me think of Kamron calling me oblivious when it comes to seeing the nuances of racism. I thought I was pretty aware of what was going on in the world and around me, but could something like racism really be in my face, and I don't know about it? How can I be knowledgeable about Black issues like Jada and Kamron?

I sigh and then head downstairs for breakfast. Sam is already here with Eric because it's driver's license day! The thought of it punches me in my gut. I'm excited to finally be a licensed driver but also nervous. What if I'm not ready? What if I need more time? What if I fail?

"Whoa!" Sam says when he looks at me.

"What?" I turn, looking at the wall behind me.

"Your hair."

"It's cute. I know." I slide my hand over the front part of my braids and wince a little. It's still tight.

"It's...different."

I sigh and walk towards the refrigerator. "Why do you hate me, Sam?"

I can feel him roll his eyes behind me, and it makes me grin. "I'm just saying. Anyway, you ready?"

"Can I eat breakfast first?" I ask, still scanning the fridge for something palatable. I don't want cereal, and I hate cooking, so I grab some frozen waffles and pop them in the toaster.

As I turn around, Coach White pops out of Mom's room. My brain takes a minute to compute it all. My seventh grade P .E. teacher smoothing his clothes, walking out of Mom's room towards the back door

"Naima. Sam," he says with a stifled wave.

"Coach White," I say because what do you say in this kind of situation? And then there's Mom in her silk robe tying it right before looking up at us.

"Goodness!" she jumps. "Why are y'all up so early?"

"Maybe we should be asking you the same thing," I say because what do you say in this kind of situation?

She sucks her teeth. "I'm grown," she whispers behind Coach White's back.

"You're not too grown to use protection," I say.

"You need to worry about yourself," she counters and walks Coach White out the door.

They stand on the porch outside the kitchen window talking. I shake my head, grab my waffles from the toaster, spread peanut butter, and drizzle honey on it.

When I turn around, Eric is staring at me with his mouth gaped open.

"What was that?"

"What was what?" I ask, chewing a bite of waffle.

"You've had sex?"

"Yeah," I shrug. He purses his lips and turns his head. "What?"

"I'm surprised. That's all."

"Why is it surprising? Everybody's had sex." I sit beside him at the kitchen bar.

"I haven't."

"It's probably different for you. I mean—" I scramble but he interrupts me.

"—Don't. Anyway, tell me—" He grabs my hands. "What was it like?"

"Normal," I say.

I had always been told that having sex was life-changing. Either the best thing I ever felt or the worst thing ever, and I'd burn in hell for it. But either way, I'd leave it feeling completely transformed. Only I didn't feel that different after the first time or second or third or however many times it's been. Don't get me wrong. Sex is as euphoric as kissing, but it just felt natural and normal and another way to show that we loved each other. If anything, it's kissing with more risk. We're one oopsie away from being parents or getting an infection.

"Did it hurt?" Eric asks, wrinkling his nose.

"No. It felt like—" I think of the word I'm trying to say. Kamron and I had talked about sex theoretically of course. We had had too many hot and heavy makeout sessions and close calls, and we wanted to be prepared for when it actually happened. Where would it be? What would we use? He thought it'd be romantic to do something out of a movie—a hotel room with rose petals and candles, but it would've been too much pressure for me to perform. I wanted authenticity. I wanted it to feel right.

"It felt right," I settle on telling him. Eric nods then smiles.

"You grown now, Cuz," he says.

"I don't feel grown." Unless being grown is feeling simultaneously underprepared for and underwhelmed by life's "milestones."

"You okay?" Eric asks but looks behind me. Turning, there's

Sam (who I completely forgot is still here) blushing near the window. I usually reserve my relationship convos for Luna. Is this the first time he's heard me talk about having sex?

"I'm fine." He waves the question away before pointing at the door. "I'll be outside when you're done."

I look down at the half a waffle I have left and stuff it in my mouth. "I'm ready."

"You're not getting peanut butter on my steering wheel."

"I'll wash my hands." I roll my eyes and rinse my hands off dramatically before drying them with a kitchen towel. Mom passes us as we walk outside. As much as I want to ask more about Coach White's sleepover, I have to focus on driver's license day.

Sam slides into the passenger seat, and I get in the driver's, adjust the seat and rear view mirror like I've done a million times before, and stick my hand out for his phone.

"What?" he asks.

"I gotta have the right sound track to get me into the mood to drive well. Otherwise, I'll fail my test, and it'll be your fault."

"My fault?" he asks, pointing the phone to his chest.

"Yeah," I grab the phone, open Spotify, and click Coco Jones's *I Didn't Tell You*.

Flicking my braids off my shoulder, I switch the dial to reverse and make my way to the county road. I'm halfway to town when I realize that I mostly drive on autopilot now. I chuckle a little remembering how tightly I gripped the wheel and how focused I used to be on keeping the car in between the lines. I used to think that driving was impossible, but I'm here doing the impossible: driving with little to no stress to me and no harm to Sam. Bless his heart. I was so close to killing us both the first few times we drove together.

When we get to the DMV, Sam reminds me to adjust my mirrors again.

"They take points off if you don't," he says. "And put your hands on ten and two and full stops at the stop signs."

"Okay, Daddy Sam," I laugh, opening the door to the building and checking in on the kiosk. When they call my name, an older white man with a clipboard waits for me by the door.

"Miss Jones?" he asks.

He opens the door for me, and I lead him to the Jeep, getting in the driver seat. Although everything is adjusted. I adjust again like Sam suggested. The man is writing on his clipboard. All I can see is the balding spot on his head as he does it so I place my hand on ten and two in preparation for the exam. When he puts his pen down, he asks, "Are you ready to get started?"

"Yes sir," I say and start the Jeep.

"Okay, we're going to back up and head towards the high-way."

I ease on my brakes to back up slow and controlled, then I place the Jeep in drive and turn onto the highway. I follow his directions driving through the neighborhood, stopping at stop signs, then turning back onto the highway. We basically drive in a large square before he instructs me to park back in the parking spot, and I do.

He finishes writing on the paper before he hands it to me. "Congratulations, Miss Jones. You're a licensed driver."

I squeal.

"Just take that to one of the clerks and get your picture taken, and you'll be on your way."

"Thank you!" I yell as he's getting out of the car.

Walking back into the DMV, I want to play it cool and keep Sam guessing, but I can't help it. A grin escapes my solemn face, and I want to jump up and down and scream, but I'm in public.

"You did it?" He whispers with a grin on his face. I nod and shake the paper in my head. I did it. I actually did it.

I hand the paper to the clerk, and when she tells me to smile, I smile the biggest smile I can make because unlike everything else, this is a hard-fought win. This feels like an actual accomplishment. I did something super hard that I struggled at for years, and I won.

Once we're outside with my license in hand, I jump up and down and squeal because I can't contain my excitement.

"I'm proud of you," Sam says before snatching the keys from me. "But I'm driving home."

I squeeze him and lay my head on his shoulder. A poof of fabric softener hits me in my face. "Thank you Sammy for teaching me and for not giving up on me and for sticking with me through all of this. I couldn't have done it without you."

He's a little hesitant about sliding an arm around me, but he does. "Yeah, don't be weird about it."

I shove his chest. "I'm not being weird. I'm being thankful."

"If you say so," he says, then grins.

On the drive back home, I watch the thick green trees past our window in a blur. I'm a high school graduate and a licensed driver soon to be a college student. Just as I'm about to get excited about the possibility, I look over at Sam driving. Now that I have my license we don't have our weekly driving lessons where I drive us to school. There's going to be no more arguing with him in the car about music. No more walking fifty feet to his house. No more us. He'll be with Dixie in California, and I'll be in college in Jackson.

I don't even notice when he parks at the house until my door opens, and his face is there. His angular face with brown curly hair. His hazel eyes squint as he smooshes his lips together.

"You alright?"

I fling myself out of the Jeep and into his arms, squeezing him.

"You're leaving," I say, smooshing my face against his neck.

"Don't think about that kind of stuff, Nai," he says, dragging his knuckles against the length of my spine in an attempt to calm me down, but I don't want to be calm. I want to be selfish and have Sam and Luna stay with me forever, but to also go to college and get away from this place.

"All I can do is think about it," I admit.

He wipes the tear from my cheek then cups my face with his hands, his fingers interlocking my braids.

"I will always be here for you," he says. His hazel eyes peer into mine, and I don't feel anxious like I usually do, but calm. Assured.

"Did you get it?" Kamron asks.

CHAPTER NINE

Kamron

Sam's holding Naima and giving her that look again. That look he gave her at the baseball field. Tears fall from her eyes, but I know she couldn't have failed her driver's test. I guess if she freaked out, she might've bombed it, but that's not like her. I still have to ask, "Did you get it?"

She jumps after I ask, and Sam lets go of her. They make me feel like I'm the outsider interloping on this special moment between them. I don't like that.

"Yeah," she says, wiping the remaining tears from her eyes. "I got my license. It's just that Sam's leaving." Her voice cracks on the word "leaving," and although Sam is already reaching out to console her, I run over to wrap my arm around her waist and bring her closer to me.

With one hand, she reaches for mine and with the other she grabs Sam's. "I think we should do something this summer before everybody leaves. This is our last summer together, and

I'm tired of crying about it. I want to make memories."

"What do you wanna do?" I ask.

She shakes her head. "I don't know yet, but maybe one thing a week where we all spend time together and do something fun."

"I'm down," Sam says.

She grins, "Okay, I'm gonna work on an itinerary and tell Luna."—Sam groans when she mentions the itinerary, but Naima continues—"Planning is for maximum funness. Is that a word? Anyway, I'll plan the fun things to do and y'all show up and have fun, okay?"

"Okay," I say at the same time, Sam says, "Got it."

She claps her hands then rushes up the porch ramp to the back door. As much as I want to ask her how the test went, I know her brain is on to the next thing so I follow her as she rushes up the stairs to her room. While she's pacing in front of the bed, I sit on it. She mouths words and a few slip out. The way she explained it is that her mind is going a mile a minute, and she needs to sort it out before she can use it. To be honest, it's kinda cute to see the way she processes anything. Her brow furrows as she bounces her finger on her lip, and I know she's trying to think, but I can't help it. I grab her hand, and she jumps from me pulling her out of her trance. Scooting back on the bed, I tug her arm to bring her closer to me until she sits on my lap and wraps her legs around me.

"Whatcha thinking?" I ask.

She playfully taps my shoulder with her finger. "You're trying to distract me."

"Is it working?"

She presses her lips against mine but stays there a bit longer, deciding. Her finger traces my bottom lip then she looks up from under her lashes. "Let me think," she whispers in her gentle tone.

I circle her waist and turn her over on the bed until I'm on top of her. She giggles. "Kamron!"

"What? I'm letting you think." I kiss her neck, and she shivers so I do it again. "Tell me what's going on."

"I wanna go swimming," she says.

I kiss the other side of her neck, and she turns her head to let me. After I kiss her there, I ask, "And what else?"

"You know the Little Big Canyon in Foxworth? Me and Sam have always wanted to go."

I raise myself up to look at her. "In this heat?"

Her shoulders slump, acquiescing, "You're right."

"What else?" I move a braid away from her face and run my finger down the length of her jaw. She leans into the touch.

"I don't know a trampoline park? Bowling?"

"I love bowling," I whisper inches from her lips.

"You do?" She reaches her hands around my neck and right as she's about to pull me closer, I stop her.

"You have to think, remember?"

She pushes me off of her while I'm laughing and then she

grabs a pillow and smacks me with it. "Why are you like this?"

"Hey," I grab her hand that's holding the pillow. "You don't have to plan the whole summer now. We can just go bowling this week and then swimming next week and then something else the next. And we don't always have to go out somewhere to hang out with each other."

She bites her lip and looks down to think it over. "Okay, that sounds like a plan."

"So, you done thinking?"

"Shut up and kiss me," she says, grabbing my face.

When I get home, Mama's suitcase is on the couch. She's meticulously folding her clothes into neat squares when she looks up at me.

"Did you break up with her yet?" she asks.

Damn, let me get in the house first. I throw my keys on the side table and head to my room.

"What?" she calls behind me. "The quicker you do it, the quicker you come home."

I don't want to go home. That's the point. I want to stay here. I sit on my bed with my head buried in my hands. I can't leave Naima. There has to be something else I can do.

When someone knocks on the door, I don't even look up to see who it is. Who cares anymore?

"Hey son," Pops says. He sits on the bed beside me.

I don't sit up to address him, just continue staring at the ceiling.

"I'm really proud of you," he says to fill in the silence. "You were barely sixteen, but you left home and created a whole new life for yourself. You've been responsible and focused even without us here to guide you, and you've made friends and your girlfriend—she's a sweet girl."

"I don't want to leave," I mumble.

"I know." He rests his hand on my knee and squeezes it. "But this is part of growing up. You do things you don't want to do, but you have to."

"Who says I have to?"

"Naima's going to college, right?" he asks. "What are you going to do?"

"Pops," I groan.

"No seriously, Kamron. What are you going to do? Are you going to college? Are you getting a job? How are you supporting yourself?"

I shake my head. "I don't know."

"Hey," Pops calls for my attention so I sit up. "I know you love her, and this is hard, but it's the best decision for both of you. She has her own future, so you have to figure out yours."

Before I can counter that she's my future, he anticipates it and says, "It's dangerous to build your future around someone else."

I try to sit with his words and chew on their meaning. What good is a future without love? What good is love if I can't have it forever? But maybe he's right. I need to start supporting myself. I don't have to go home and keep relying on the allowance my parents give me, I can get a job and stay in Mississippi. Then I don't have to break up with Naima. We can stay together and one day, get married. I look up at Pops then with a smile on my face. Now, I have a plan.

"Can you give me til the end of summer to find a job?"

He exhales and tightens his mouth like he doesn't want to give in but then decides to. "This is your last extension. I'm giving you til July. If you can't find one by then, you're coming home."

"Thanks Pops," I wrap my arm around him, hugging him. He hugs me back.

"Love you son."

"Love you, too, Pops."

"Alright." He pats my shoulder as he stands. "We're gonna finish packing and head up to Memphis. Talk to your mother for me?"

"Okay," I say as he shuts the door behind him.

I give myself a few more minutes before walking back into the living room. Mama's there zipping up her leather suitcases.

"Hey Mama," I lean against the wall, waiting for her to finish.

"Oh, Kam." She rushes over and hugs me then kisses my

cheek. She runs her head over my cornrows before commenting, "You're really committed to this?"

I move my head away from her hand. Her hair is straight from some kind of Japanese treatment she does to it, but she's constantly fussed at me and Jada for growing ours out naturally.

"I like it like this."

"I hope you're not gonna get dreadlocks or something?" She shudders.

"Mama."

"I just want you to look your best." Her palm presses against my cheek while she looks at me for a moment. I expect her to have an honest conversation with me, but instead she says, "I made you a doctor's appointment."

"What?"

"You've been here for two years and haven't been to the doctor? It's on your birthday."

"Wait, what? What if I had plans for my birthday?"

"What plans? Are you going to spend it with that country bumpkin?"

There it is.

"Mama," I exhale trying to wrestle control of this conversation.

"I almost made a dentist appointment, but you can see Dr. Filoni when you get back." She grabs the handles on her suitcases and drags them to the door. On the side table, she picks up one of my sculptures.

"I saw your art in your studio." My jaw clenches. My studio is a sacred and *private* space. "I can talk to Peri if you're interested in an apprenticeship."

Periwinkle Moonchild (she legally changed it to that) is a renowned potter in Northern California. She's exhibited all over the world. Working under her could really boost my profile in the art world. It'd also help me feel better about the mounting rejections I've gotten. Five so far.

"Thank you," I say, hesitantly. Knowing Mama, there's a catch.

She nods and then calls Pops to help her put the bags in their rental car. Jada rolls her suitcase out of Amaya's room where she was staying.

"Bye baby brother," she says, hugging me. "I'll keep them off your back."

"Thank you."

"She's good for you, and she's crazy about you. When I was doing her hair, she was going on and on and on and on—" I start laughing and then she joins in. "But I'm happy for you. Have a good summer with her."

"I'll try."

She hugs me again before walking out the door. I stand in the doorway watching them pull off and wave at them.

Eighty-seven days until Naima goes to college, and now forty-one days to get a job.

Chapter Ten
Group Chat

Best Summer Ever

SAM: What is this?

NAIMA: It's the best summer ever

Wait

SAM: Is this your itinerary thing

We're all leaving after this summer so I made a bucket list of ways to spend time together before everyone leaves. Sam and Kamron already agreed so I'm waiting on you, Luna.

LUNA: Waiting on me for what?

Yes this is about the itinerary

To have the best summer ever

LUNA: What does that mean??!

Kamron and I wanted to go bowling this Friday and then go swimming next week.

LUNA: This Friday? Before or after our bbq?

I totally didn't forget about the bbq. I was gonna say we can go bowling Satur-day

SAM: Where's the nearest bowling alley and can Dixie come

There's one in Philadelphia. Like 40 min away.

Yeah she can come

KAMRON: Where are we meeting at?

We can meet at your place.

3 Saturday?

I'll send calendar invites

LUNA: We don't need them!!!

KAMRON: Thank you baby

LUNA: Kamron don't start

Chapter Eleven

Naima

When I go downstairs, Mom's standing in the kitchen on her phone. My footsteps slow as I think about how to approach the whole Coach White in our house thing. She looks up from her phone at me, and I glance from side to side.

"You don't have another one of my teachers hiding out in here?" I joke.

She forcefully exhales. "Very funny, Naima."

I giggle sliding onto the bar stool. "I'm not mad or any-thing...I'm just...surprised."

It's been almost four years since Dad died. I miss him, and the love we have for him will never go away, but over the years, we've learned to live around his absence. Mom's dated no one since. I'm not silly enough to believe in soul mates. That there's eight billion people on this planet and only one true love for you? That seems statistically unlikely, but it's still surprising that Mom will break that streak for Coach White of all people. He's nothing like Dad. Dad was tall and lanky, a little bit nerdy. Coach White is all muscle-ly and when we had P.E., he was more focused on his workout than ours.

"Quinten and I are just friends."

I lift my eyebrows and widen my eyes.

"Don't give me that look," she scolds. "It's not serious."

I raise both my palms. "I get it. You're a person and you have...needs. It's just gross to think about."

"It's equally uncomfortable to think about my own daughter having *needs*."

"You were my age once," I shrug. "I've never been old...like you."

"Watch it," she warns and I giggle. "I'm still a hottie or whatever you call it."

"Sure you are, Mom."

She laughs and then I join her. It's hard to remember the years when Mom used to be so hard on me, and I thought she hated me. Now she treats me like my own person, and as gross as it is to think about, I have to treat her like her own person as well...needs and all.

"Just don't tell your brother," she says soberly. "He may not take it as well as you."

Markese is thirteen now and will start eighth grade in a few months so he'll still be in the same school as Mom and Coach White. Knowing about the two of them may be too much for his baby brain.

"Don't worry. I won't," I reassure her. "Anyway, the Hernandezes are having a barbecue today. I was wondering if I could take the car."

"That's right. You're Little Miss Licensed Driver now."

I swipe my braids off my shoulder to hype myself up. She squints her eyes, "Is Sam not going?"

"He's not."

"Fine." She searches in the junk drawer. "Here's the spare. Be home before dark and drive safe."

I kiss her on her cheek. "Thanks, Mom. I will."

In her Chevy Equinox, I adjust the seat, steering wheel, and mirror. Sam's Jeep is in the rearview mirror, and it squeezes my heart. This is my first time driving without anyone but especially without him. I look over to the empty passenger seat and sigh. This is growing up, I guess. Being independent and doing things alone. No time for tears.

I play "No Time for Tears" by Little Mix and turn out of the driveway headed for town. For a song about moving on and being defiant by not crying when others expect you to, it doesn't cheer me up like I hope it would. I pull behind a car on the road near Luna's house and walk up to her doorway.

Mr. Hernandez spots me first. "¡Wepa! ¡Wepa!" he calls while doing a little foot shuffle. I dance along with him. He wraps an arm around my shoulder. "I see you on the stage with your little yellow sash. Eres lista."

"Gracias." I smile.

"Now Luna. I ask where's her little sash and she's like—" He sticks his lips out and shrugs his shoulders in exaggerated confusion. I laugh because although I know I can be dramatic, Mr. Hernandez is more so.

When I start to settle down, I ask, "Are you excited about going back to Mexico?"

"Yes, very. Beautiful country. Have you been?"

"No, I haven't."

His mouth gapes open. "You have to come. You'll love it. The singing y dancing y comida."

"Ah, la comida."

"Sí. Es rica. You'll love it."

"Do you have any family there?" I ask. "Or are they all still in Puerto Rico?"

"Eh, since Maria, a lot more of them moved away."

Uh-oh. This is the part of the conversation that I don't know how to transition away from or keep going so I stay silent hoping that he'll change the subject or something.

Thankfully, Mrs. Hernandez comes handing Mr. Hernandez seasoned meat for the grill. Standing next to each other, they're similar heights and similar shades of honey-brown. Luna has round cheekbones like her mother and her father's round face and peachy lips. Although Luna has her mother's raven black hair, Luna's has a slight wave whereas her mom's is bone straight. Being of mixed heritage, Luna says that she got the best of both worlds, and for the most part I'd agree, especially when it comes to the food. There was that one time I walked in on her parents having a heated debate over the correct way to say "beans" in Spanish, and I learned to say "habichuelas" for Mr. Hernandez and "frijoles" for literally the rest of the world.

Mr. Hernandez takes the tray and excuses himself. Mrs. Hernandez says hey to me and tells me that Luna is still in her room. Walking into her room, I'm welcomed by the elongated screech of her black cat, Nellie.

"Hello, Gatita." I pick her lithe body up, and she curls into my arms like a baby. I rock her, and she slow blinks at me. Slow blinks mean they love you.

"Ugh," Luna groans. "You're so dressed up. Now I have to dress up."

She's brushing out her hair. I look down at my yellow sundress I'm wearing, and my palm tree Crocs with tan socks. Not my idea of dressing up, but thanks to Jada, having a braided hairstyle automatically elevates whatever I'm wearing. I sit on the bed with Nellie and stroke her fur while Luna scurries around her room looking for a change of clothes. She settles on a floral blouse, blue jean shorts, and a ponytail.

When we walk outside, the party has doubled. The smell of grilled meat and humidity hangs in the air while Latin music plays from speakers. I follow Luna to the food table, load up a plate with skewered meat, corn, and plátanos then sit. As we sit, her play cousins, Crystal and Nacho, are fighting over a toy. They're speaking in Spanglish. When the rapid-fire Spanish comes, I can catch a word here or there. My brain usually lags when I hear people speak in English—my native language—hearing Spanish is a nightmare for me unless they speak *lentamente*.

"Give it back to me, you chicken nugget," Crystal says.

I laugh, and Crystal stares at me, her tiny lip quirking that I found her funny.

"I'm stealing that," I whisper to Luna whose attention is glued to her phone.

"What?" she says.

"The chicken nugget thing. Are you listening?"

"No I—" She puts the phone down disgruntled. As much as I don't want it to be Ricky, I know it is. I've never even met the guy, but I already know he has the worst effect on her.

"Anyway," she changes the subject. "Why do you wanna go bowling tomorrow?"

"I've never been."

"You've never been? How have you—" She thinks about it. "Yep, you've never came with us."

"It'll be my first time. I'm a bowling virgin, but it'll be fun."

"Yeah, I guess." She gnaws on her lip and glances at her phone.

"Anyway, Dixie will be there." I say and Luna gives me a look. "How many times will she be like 'Sam, we have to take a picture. No like this. No like *this*'?"

Luna emits a small laugh. "She's always 'Video this. Video that.'"

"I just—" I sigh. It feels like she's using him for his followers to grow her account and not because she actually likes Sam. I think Sam deserves better than that.

"What does he see in her?" Luna asks the question circling my mind.

"I wish I could see it," I tell her. "Anyway, guess who was in my house the other day?"

"Who?" she asks, scrunching her eyebrows.

"Coach White," I widen my eyes to show my shock.

She shakes her head. "Why?"

"Apparently him and Mom are 'just friends.'" I gesture a hole with one hand and stick my finger into it.

Her mouth gapes open. "Go Mama Jones."

I laugh then Luna asks, "Are you okay with it?"

"If she's happy, I'm happy. I'm happy for her."

Luna nods then a smile crosses her face as she looks past me. When I turn, there's Ricky, her situationship. He came.

Great.

Ricky's tall and extremely beautiful. Honestly, I don't know where Luna finds these boys she dates. They're all the most attractive boys I've ever seen in my life. But that's all Ricky has to offer. I'm not saying Luna doesn't have great taste in boys, but they've all been shitty to her. Even the one I liked the most, Kike, he would tell her how much better she would look if she lost weight. Asshole. She's absolutely perfect the way she is. Always. But Ricky shows up when he wants, makes this grand gesture to Luna, then forgets she exists for weeks. It's a cycle, but again, he's not her boyfriend, but she's "his girl," and if she thinks about being with anyone else, he freaks out.

I hate him.

He slides between me and Luna, wraps his arm around her shoulder, and asks, "Natalie, right?"

Who the fuck is Natalie?

"Naima," I squint my eyes and stifle my frown.

"Right, right," he turns to Luna. "Hey babe, can you fix me a plate? I haven't eaten all day." He rubs his belly to really emphasize it.

She smiles. "Of course. Be right back."

He leans backwards on the bench, spreading his arms and legs wide, like the world is his and he's allowed to take up as much space as he likes.

"You graduate with her, right?" he asks.

I nod.

"Y'all friends are something?"

I nod again.

"You don't smile or nothing? I think you'd look so much prettier if you did." He puts his thumb on my lips and tries to drag it down, staring at me with fuel in his eyes. It feels gross. I don't know why, but my body refuses to move. My teeth clench, and my whole inside vibrates with anger.

"—here's your plate," Luna drops it in front of him, and he slides away from me.

"What's wrong with your friend? She don't talk or nothing?"

"Leave," she says, her voice firm and even.

"What?" he chuckles. "I can't ask you about your friend?"

"Leave!" She raises her voice, slamming the plate she just made into his shirt. A few heads turn our way, and I'm embarrassed that I was part of making this a huge scene.

"You bitch!" he yells.

"Fuck you!" she yells back. People stare at us, but Luna's glare is reserved for Ricky. "Go!"

He backs up hesitantly, looking down at his dirty shirt, then he storms off. Luna drops onto the bench and covers her face with her hands.

"I'm sorry," I place my hand on her shoulder, hoping it soothes her. "I didn't—I shouldn't." Maybe I should've just talked to him but being near him made me feel oily and disgusting and gross.

"No, I'm sorry. I'm the reason he's here." She shakes her head and then looks at the table. "I didn't like the way he touched you. It just kinda clicked then. Like he's not going to get any better. I'm so stupid."

"You're not," I rush to say. She's a million great and amazing things. Fuck Ricky for making her question herself.

"It took me so long to see." She throws her hands in the air.

"Why can't I find one good guy?"

"Boys are pointless. Who wants one, anyway?" I ask, trying to lighten her mood. She stares at me because I have an amazing boyfriend and have been extremely lucky to have such a successful first relationship. I smile then she laughs.

"No more dating for me," she decides. "Maybe Mexico has better boys, and it's just Mississippi boys that are trash."

Mexico. I twiddle my thumbs. She's leaving in five weeks. I exhale and change the subject.

"But before you leave we have our best summer ever and tomorrow we're going bowling, remember?" I bump my shoulder against hers.

"Yeah," she smiles. "At least I still have you."

Chapter Twelve

Naima

"Take your brother," Mom says. This was supposed to be a fun outing with friends, and now I have to babysit plus Dixie will be there. I groan, and Mom puts her hand up. "Nope. I don't want to hear it. He needs to get out of the house."

"Fine," I say and yell up the stairs for him to come down. "I hope you're not gonna be hoe-hopping while we're gone."

"What *I* do in *my* house is none of *your* business." Mom tries to frown, but a smirk tugs on the corner of her lips. I squint at her.

"Well we'll try and stay out til about six if that's enough time for you."

"That should be fine." She gazes at her fingers, and I shake my head.

Markese hurries down the stairs in a t-shirt and basketball shorts. As predicted, Markese is taller than both of us. At thirteen years old, he's six feet tall. Every time he stands next to me, he towers over me, and I want to cry. What happened to the little toddler that I used to try and pick up when I was seven? Now he can pick me up.

He shoves me. "Come on, Lil Dip." And his voice deepened. I'm not emotionally prepared for any of this.

When we walk outside, Sam and Dixie wait for us in the driveway. We hop in the backseat of the Jeep and head to Kamron's house. There, he and Luna lean up against his Prius talking. I leap out of the car and into his arms. A mix of sweat, citrus, and lavender greet me when I nuzzle my face into his neck. He kisses my forehead.

"How are we doing this?" Sam asks.

"I'm going with Sam," Markese says, raising his hand.

Of course he is. He thinks the world revolves around Sam. Although Markese plays football, he started playing baseball this past year because Sam did, and they got to practice together. He's basically living out his fantasies of having Sam as his big brother.

"I'll stay with these two," Luna says, and we split up. Kamron trails Sam to Philadelphia. I sit with Luna on the backseat, singing along to Karol G, Melii, and Goyo. There are times where Kamron peeks at us in the rearview mirror and smiles.

For Memorial Day weekend, the bowling alley is packed. Luckily there are a couple of open lanes, and we reached the maximum of six people per lane. As we're putting on our shoes, Kamron says, "I can't believe you've never bowled. I used to be in a bowling league in fourth grade."

"A what?" I ask.

"A bowling league. We bowled every Wednesday after school."

First Little League and now bowling. What kind of secret athletic childhood did he have?

"Are you gonna whoop us?" I groan.

"Nah. I'll go easy on y'all," he says. Amusement tugs on his beautiful lips.

Luna enters our names on the screen putting Markese down first then Sam, Dixie, herself, me, and Kamron last. None of us want the added pressure of going after the bowling superstar.

When Dixie gets up to bowl, Sam videos her. He follows her with the camera, taking videos from several different angles. The whole time she's standing there with the ball pretending to bowl. When she gets a shot she likes, she finally bowls the ball. And that's just her first shot. She takes the same amount of time to take her second shot. Luna and I look at each other at the same time and purse our lips. When she finally bowls, she's knocked down eight pins total. Not bad, but she could've done it quicker.

"Sorry y'all," she says. "I think that's enough filming for the day."

I think so, too.

Luna drops her ball on the lane. It slowly rolls until it goes into the gutters. "Can I get the things?" she asks, making rows with her hands. She fiddles with the screen until bars come out on the edges of the lane.

"I want that too," I tell her.

"You don't need it. Just bowl like the rest of us," Sam teases.

"Shut up," I say to him.

Luna bowls again, and this time hits a few pins. I clap for her before getting up for my turn. Nerves bumble around in my stomach when I realize that everyone is looking at me, and I have to perform. With the bumpers still up, I throw the ball down the lane, knocking a couple of pins down. I twirl around clapping, grab the ball again, and throw it quickly so I can sit down. It rolls and hits a few more pins. When I sit beside Luna and look at the screen overhead, it shows that we both have five.

"We're tied," I say, high-fiving her.

Kamron rises and rubs his palms together. He places his knuckles in front of the vent. For what? I don't know, but he selects his ball, testing its weight in his hand. Then he puts his feet together near the center of the lane and in one fell swoop, shoots the ball down the aisle. It knocks down every pin. My mouth drops and Luna says, "What the—"

"We bout to lose!" Markese throws his hands in the air.

Sam shakes his head, and Dixie is surprisingly giddy. Kamron just shrugs and smiles as he returns to his seat.

"What happened to going easy on us?" I ask.

"Next frame?" He places his hand on my knee and grins. We're getting stomped.

When it's my turn again, I make Kamron tutor me. He places his hand on my ball. "How does it feel to hold this?"

"It feels fine?" I'm not sure what he wants me to say.

"Is it heavy? Are your fingers snug?"

I bounce the ball, and it feels a little light, and my fingers are a little too snug so I tell him.

"Try this ball." He hands me another ball and it's heavier, but not too heavy, and my fingers are snug, but not too snug. I nod so he positions me in the center of the lane. Then beside me, he slows down his throwing motion so I can copy him. "Like this," he says.

I practice keeping one foot still, slightly lifting the other and then sliding the ball before I actually let it go. It stays in the middle and hits at least half of them. I bounce around clapping that I got it right.

"Just keep doing that, and you'll get it," Kamron tells me before slipping back into his seat. I try again and knock down a few more pins. When I look at the screen, it says I got eight. Better than the first round.

Kamron bowls a turkey? Idk what that means, but he's in the lead by *a lot*. By the sixth round, I got the swing of how to bowl. My first chance, I knock a good bit down. The two corner ones are left standing. I kinda angle my body towards those two pins and throw the ball.

"Please, please, please," I tell it as it heads towards the pins. It rolls slowly, hits one, and then that pin hits the other.

"I did it! I did it!" I jump around to celebrate, and Kamron wraps his arms around my waist. I kiss his cheeks. "I did it."

"You did," he grins.

"You're such a good teacher."

"I know," he chuckles.

"You're great at everything. You're smart...and beautiful...and talented...and—" With each compliment, I pepper his face with kisses.

"Get a room!" Luna heckles.

"Yeah, quit being disgusting," Markese joins in.

"Shut up," I say. "Y'all hate love." I turn my attention back to Kamron whose face softens in my hands. He squeezes my waist before grabbing his ball to and knocking down nine pins.

Kamron wins the first game. Of course. Surprisingly, Dixie is second, me third, Markese fourth, Sam fifth and Luna last. We order pizza before starting our second game. Sitting around the table, Dixie videos herself eating pizza because what doesn't she video herself doing? As I'm eating my slice, I see Luna's phone lights up. In my peripheral I see the text: *Plz talk to me* and know it's from Ricky.

Luna looks at the phone then me and swallows. "I'm sorry again about yesterday. I told him it was over."

"What happened yesterday?" Kamron asks, and Luna and I look at each other. I didn't tell Kamron because I didn't think to tell Kamron. I just didn't want to think about it again.

"Ricky assaulted her," Luna says.

"He what?!" He slams the pizza down, wipes his hand, and then holds my face, searching it for some injury. I bury my head because I don't want to see him looking at me with pity-filled eyes.

"Assault sounds extreme. He just grabbed my face."

"Without your permission. That's assault, Naima," Luna says, softly.

My eyes reach Kamron's, and I can see the exact moment that the truth of it breaks his heart.

"I'm fine," I reassure him. "It was nothing."

"It's not nothing," he says. His fists ball in his lap. His lips narrow into a line, and his jaw clenches. I reach out and caress his jagged jawline with my thumb to soften the tension. I don't want him to worry about me.

"It's not nothing, okay? But I'm fine. See?" I take one of his fists, unclench it, and place his palm on my cheek. I want his touch to undo the harshness of Ricky's from yesterday. The steel in his eyes slowly melts away, and I grab his palm and kiss it.

"I'm okay, seriously. Luna cussed him out and protected me." I hold onto her hand, too. "I'm perfectly fine because I have both of you."

I smile at them, but neither of them return it.

Chapter Thirteen

Kamron

I'm perfectly fine because I have both of you.

Her words have been repeating in my head ever since Saturday. She won't have Luna forever, and unless I can find a job this summer, she won't have me either. If we both leave, what will she do? Who will be there to protect her from guys like Ricky? She'll be alone, and it'll be my fault because I failed her and couldn't find a way to stay in Mississippi.

I stare at the resume template and realize that I have no experience, no extracurriculars, nothing except honors and good grades which means I know how to take a test, not that I know how to work a job. Despite Naima's insistence, I've learned that I'm actually great at nothing. I rest my head on my palm staring at the laptop screen. What have I done with my life?

I don't know how long I've been staring at the screen when Amaya knocks on the door.

"You doing okay?" she asks.

I turn the laptop around to face her. "Working on my resume."

She glances at the blank screen then back to me. Plopping on the foot of the bed she offers, "You can work with me at the shop, and be my apprentice."

Amaya's a mechanic and a damn good one. She's known for quality work and fair pricing, for both her and the customer.

"What do apprentices do?" I ask.

She tilts her head side to side thinking about how to explain it. "Clean. But it's minimum wage," she rushes to say. "Seeing as you live here for free, I don't think that's a bad deal."

I flip the laptop back at me and stare at the screen. "I was thinking of living in Jackson," I admit. I haven't had the whole "I want to move out" talk with her. I love Amaya. She's my favorite aunt, and I've loved living with her, but I'm going to be eighteen soon, and I want to feel like an adult which means living on my own.

"Oh." Sadness crosses her face, and I feel like an asshole.

"I've loved living here, don't get me wrong." She's given me half of her house to live and create art out of. "I just think—"

"You want to be grown?" she finishes for me.

"Yeah," I admit.

She nods, coming to terms with what I said so I breathe a sigh of relief. Everything is out in the open with her now.

"Well if I were you, I wouldn't worry too much about a

resume. Since you're right out of high school, most places will know that you don't have much experience so you shouldn't have too much of a problem finding a job, even in Jackson."

"Thanks," I say.

"Yeah." Her lips thin into a line. "Let me know if you need help with anything."

I tell her I will before she leaves me with the computer screen. Instead of completing a resume, I search for jobs with no experience in Jackson. Most are driving jobs—delivery and CDL. I keep scrolling and there's sales, retail, and a few factory jobs. There's an entry level automotive technician with basic experience. Despite living with Amaya for the past two years, I can't do any kind of car work. She's done all my maintenance. I settle on the help desk specialist, office coordinator, and medical office jobs. I apply to all three before getting dressed and hope one of them will let me find a way to stay in Mississippi.

After spending the day at Nana's for her Memorial Day lunch and driving back from the Delta, I'm exhausted, but Naima is still on my mind. I want to check up on her, make sure she's doing okay. I know she'll claim she is, but I have to see for myself.

Laying on my bed, I video call her. It takes a few rings before her beautiful face fills the screen. Her braids are wrapped in her scarf, and she's laying on her pillow, rubbing her eye. It is late for her, almost nine, so I wouldn't be surprised if she's going to bed now.

"Hey," I say, watching her through the screen wondering if her fatigue will let some emotion slip through.

"Hey," she yawns, sitting the phone down on her nightstand and laying on her hands to look at me. I smile because of how perfect and peaceful she looks. It reminds me of when I read to her, and she fell asleep on my chest. After a while, I just sat there and watched her, committing the sight to memory.

"Is something wrong?" she asks. Worry creases her brows.

"No," I shrug. "Just wanted to check up on you. See if you're doing okay."

"I'm fine," she says, her usual reply. Her eyes travel towards the ceiling, and she sighs. She's not fine. She turns back to me and changes the subject. "What about you? Your birthday's around the corner. Any big plans?"

"I have a doctor's appointment," I admit.

"Oh." Her voice is soft as her doe-eyes widen. She's adorable.

"In Jackson," I add.

"Is it bad?" Her nose scrunches up.

I hope it isn't, but I guess that's for the doctor to decide.

"It's just a check-up," I reassure her. "Mama scheduled it before she left."

"On your birthday?" she asks.

"She didn't want me to forget."

"Well if you're tired, you don't have to come here. I don't want you stressing yourself out."

It's cute that she extends the same courtesy to me that she

needs for herself.

"All I want for my birthday is to see you," I smile, and her smile encourages and saddens me at the same time. If I can't get a job, I won't have her forever, but at least I have her for now.

"Okay. I can do that." She nods slightly then bites her lips. The humor that filled her face quickly vanishes and then her eyes turn back to me. "I'm sorry I didn't tell you about Ricky," she mumbles.

My anger towards him makes itself known when it rises up in my chest. "*You* have nothing to be sorry about," I remind her. *He* has a lot to be sorry about.

"I just wanted to forget it happened. I felt...I don't know—powerless in that moment, and I hated it. I hated him, and I just—I hated that it even happened at all."

"I felt powerless, too," I admit.

"You did?" she asks, her eyes focus on the screen, staring at me.

"Yeah, when you told me," I say. "It made me so angry, and there was nothing I could do to help you."

She silently watches me, her face blank and her eyes wide.

"I hate seeing you hurt," I confess and what makes it worse is that if I fail this summer, I'll be the next one to hurt her.

CHAPTER FOURTEEN

Naima

Luna's been super apologetic about Ricky since the bbq. I keep telling her it's fine, but she keeps going on and on about how sorry she is. Like Kamron, they're both so worried about me which makes me wonder if it's a bigger deal than I realize. Sure, it felt uncomfortable to be around Ricky, and hopefully I never have to see him again, but it feels like they're making this a bigger deal than it is. Is this what Kamron means when he said I was oblivious to everything?

"Are you okay?" Luna quits her apology tour and slides over on her bed to look right into my eyes. Although I've been stroking Nellie's side, Luna's hands clasp my free hand, and I hold onto hers.

"I'm fine. I told you a million times."

Sadness fills her eyes, and guilt tugs on my heart. If anything, I'm worried about her. My first time seeing Ricky irl was enough for me to never want to see him again. She's been with him for months now. Is *she* okay? Nellie shifts in my lap so I stroke the top of her head. She mews and closes her eyes to slits, enjoying the tiny pets.

"Are you okay?" I ask her exactly what's on my mind.

Luna leans back, crosses her arms over her chest, and averts her gaze. Before she can say anything, her phone buzzes on her nightstand. She looks at it, then me, before picking it up. Her expression immediately contorts. Her nose and mouth scrunches in disgust, and I know before she can say anything who it is. She huffs and angrily types out a response. When she sends it, she turns her phone over and drops her head in her lap.

"What is it?" I ask, petting Nellie, bracing for the worst.

"It's nothing," she mumbles.

"It's Ricky," I say, letting her know that she can talk to me. I don't care about Ricky, but I do care about her.

"It's—" she starts. "He—" and then she shows me the text. He's saying she's overreacting and calling her a baby. He's trying to make it seem like she's the problem for saying something and not that he's the problem for doing something.

I put Nellie down on the floor. She grumbles and protests, but this is serious. Placing my hand on Luna's thigh, I reassure her, "It's not your fault."

"I know that!" she yells but when she realizes what she's done she lowers her voice. "I know that. Why am I so broken that I can't have a normal relationship? You have Kamron. Sam has Dixie. I have no one."

"You have me," I remind her.

"It's not the same."

But why not? Without Kamron, Luna has always been enough for me. I love her with everything inside of me. Why can't I be enough for her? Maybe she sees the hurt building inside of me because she apologizes.

"I'm sorry. I do love you. It's just that I want to have somebody, too. Somebody that makes me feel like I'm enough. Somebody that's not an asshole." She wipes a tear and gestures towards her phone to the asshole in question.

I grab her hand. "You will find your somebody. You're hot and beautiful, and you have a fat ass" —she laughs with that one— "You're funny and kind and great at makeup and every amazing thing under the sun."

She offers a sad smile. "Maybe I am half of them. My ass isn't that fat."

"You have the fattest ass I've ever seen," I tell her. "And you're everything that's great in the world."

A lone tear falls down her pink cheeks, "Thank you, Naima."

"I love you so much, and I hate Ricky for making you feel this way," I confess to her. He's a loser because there's no part of her that can ever be unlovable. I want to hit him with a baseball bat for making her feel like she is.

Luna wraps her arm around my neck and pulls me in for a

hug. I rub her back and try to change the subject to make her feel better. "What's the one thing you always wanted to do in Mississippi?"

She breaks the hug and sits back to think about it. Finally Luna shrugs. "I don't know. I always wanted to get another piercing, but I can do that anywhere."

"A piercing?" I think about it. My mom's like most Southern Black moms and pierced my ears in infancy so I don't even remember it. I've never consented to any piercings in my life.

"Yeah, like a nose piercing." She looks over at my nose. "You have a perfect nose for a piercing."

"I do?"

"Yeah." She sniffles and touches my left nostril. "Right there, you'd look so cute."

"I already look cute," I joke, and she laughs which makes my heart swell.

"Okay, but cuter. You should get it, girl."

I chew my bottom lip. Piercings are so final. I mean I could take it out if it doesn't look right, but I'm Black so there's always the chance of keloids, and I saw this man once who had these huge keloids on his ears from his piercings, and what if my nose looks like that? What if I need surgery from a botched piercing and what if—

"Hey," Luna calls my attention. "Don't overthink it."

"Too late." I'm already thinking about the worst possible scenario.

"You don't have to get a piercing. I can get one whenever."

"Does it hurt?" I ask her.

She has three in each ear. One from infancy and the other two when we were fifteen and sixteen.

She shrugs, "It's a little pinch, but like I said if you don't want to, you don't have to."

Chapter Fifteen

Kamron

It's been five minutes since Luna texted that she'd come out so we can meet up at Naima's to go swimming, and I'm still waiting. When she finally does open the door, tears stream her round face and rosy cheeks. She shuffles into the car with her bag.

"Sorry about that," she says.

"You okay?"

She dismisses my concern with a wave. "No, it's fine."

I shift towards her. "We can talk about it if you need to," I offer. Something's obviously wrong. Why are girls always trying to pretend like it's not?

She glances at me hard. Like she's trying to make up her mind about whether or not she wants to talk to me before she decides to. "What the hell. It's Ricky."

My jaw clenches automatically when I hear his name.

"He just called me *begging* to see me, and when I said no, he called me a bitch and a slut. I don't get it. He made it seem like I was so lucky that he *chose* me. Ugh!" She buries her face in her hands. "What's wrong with me?"

"Hey." I gently pat her shoulder. "Nothing's wrong with you. Ricky's the problem. He's red flag after red flag."

She leans her head back against the headrest and sniffles. "I know. I have *great* taste in boys."

I smile sympathetically as she rolls her head towards me. "Please don't tell Naima about this. I already feel bad that I'm still texting him."

"I won't," I reassure her then back out of her driveway to head to Naima's. By the time we get there, Luna's tears have dried up, and Sam's Jeep is in the driveway with him and Naima standing beside it.

"Just the four of us?" I ask.

"Yeah, Dixie's not coming. Eric is never here. I don't know where that boy goes, and Mom isn't forcing me to take Markese so I'm free," Naima says, smiling at the last part.

"Cool, you want me to drive?" I ask.

She juts her thumb at Sam. "He's driving."

He jangles his keys in the air with a smug look on his face.

"Do y'all need sunscreen? I already applied," she asks.

"Ooh me," Luna says, her earlier turmoil already dissipated.

"I'll wait til we get there," Sam says.

"You're the main one that needs sunscreen," Naima says, staring at Sam.

"What's that supposed to mean?"

She grins then grabs the sunscreen out of the truck to spray Luna.

"Sunscreen?" Naima asks me.

"Nah, I'll apply in the car," I tell her. She turns, but I grab her hand and whirl her around towards me. "Hey," I say once I'm inches from her lips.

"Hey." She grins back at me then kisses me, rubbing her finger across my cheek. Her gaze scans my face before she asks, "You ready to go?"

"Yeah," I say. I just had to check in with her real quick. As she turns away, a pained look crosses Sam's face. That's weird, but I throw my stuff in the trunk and ignore it. I'm about to get into the backseat with Naima when she asks me to get in the front.

"It's just that I want to sit by Luna unless you want all of us to squeeze back here. Sam, you wanna be our chauffeur?" she jokes.

I glance at Luna, and she offers me a small nod. A gentle okay that she needs this as much as Naima wants it.

"No chauffeuring. I'll get in the front," I say and slide in the passenger seat beside Sam.

"You wanna DJ?" he asks, handing me his phone.

Naima gasps. "Why do I have to fight you for the music?"

"Because all you play is Little Mix."

"That's not all I play!"

"Okay, okay," I mediate between them. "What's something everybody wants to hear?"

"I just want something that's bright and summery," Naima says.

"Me too!" Luna adds.

"No pop music," Sam says to me but loud enough for Naima to hear.

Naima screeches in the back seat.

"That's my only rule," Sam says to her in the rearview mirror.

She crosses her arms in the backseat and pouts.

"Fine. Luna, what's that Melii song? Da-da-da-da Da-da-da-da Da-da loca?" Naima asks.

"Como Si Na?"

How do they do that?

Naima snaps. "Yeah, play 'Como Si Na' by Melii."

I search for it and play the Spotify radio for the song. "Okay let me know if y'all have any other requests. I'll queue them."

As the song plays, Naima tries to keep up with the Spanish and fails. Luna laughs at her at certain points. My Spanish isn't as great as it was back in California when I was immersed in the language, and Dominican Spanish is...different, but from what I get, the song is about a woman in love with a man who enjoys hurting her. Maybe not the best song for Luna to listen to, but when you don't know what the lyrics say, it's a vibe.

I queue Leigh-Anne's song with Arya Starr. It's not technically Little Mix, but I know she'll appreciate it. When the song starts, Naima gasps, shaking my seat and smiling at me. For a second she looks in my eyes, gratitude filling them before she sings and dances along to the song in the back seat. It's moments like that that I want forever.

I play a mix of afrobeats and Latin music to keep the vibe going until we get to a water park. When Naima said swimming, I assumed she meant a pool, but it's a full on water park with slides, a lazy river, and a wave pool.

"A water park?" Luna asks.

"Yeah, I was talking with Sam this morning, and he suggested Geyser Falls instead of the nearest swimming pool since we had to drive so far to get to either," Naima says.

"It's badass. I love it." I look over the seat to smile at her. She grins back at me.

When I open the door, the heat and humidity swarm me. We grab our bags, pay, then by the time we're inside, a sweat has already started to build up. We stand off to the side to decide our action plan for the day. The lazy river courses on one side of us and a huge slide called "Backwash" is on our other side.

"So how are we doing this?" Naima asks, gesturing at the park.

"I'm thinking we do the slides first since they tend to have the longest lines," I suggest. I went to a water park a couple of times as a kid, and that was always how our family did it.

Naima looks to everyone to see if they're okay with that

suggestion. When everyone nods, Naima claps. "Perfect! We have a plan."

We rent a locker to store our clothes and phones. Naima takes off her dress to reveal a one-piece swimsuit that conforms to her curves and dips at her chest and her back. She's stuffing her dress in the locker when Sam says, "I'm ready for sunscreen."

"Spray or lotion?" Naima asks.

"You know Coach says the spray is bad for you. It don't spray evenly so it can give you cancer."

Naima stares at him. Her face is frozen. "Why did you tell me that when I'm tryna have a good time? Now I have to reapply."

Sam shrugs and grabs the sunscreen to apply it. He takes his shirt off, and dude's ripped. Here I am with stretch marks on my belly. He hands the bottle to Naima and points to his back. She squirts a lot into her hands and smooths it onto his back. It looks sensual how she rubs it into every crevice and plays close attention to his neck and shoulders. I can't lie, I'm jealous. Does she wish I had a body like that? Does she want to be with someone that looks like him?

Nah, I'm tripping, but then she hands the bottle to him, slips her straps off her shoulders, and moves her braids out of the way to rub sunscreen onto her back.

"I got it," I jog over and grab the bottle from Sam. He backs out of my way, and after I use the sunscreen, he grabs the bottle and asks Luna to apply it to his face. I don't know why he didn't ask Luna to start with.

The line for Whitewater Express isn't that long. It's a waterslide that doubles as a race. Once we're a few feet away from the start, we grab blue foam pads and then line up. There's a person waiting there so we split the party. Naima and Luna decide to go first. Then Sam, me, and a little white boy line up for us to go. We lay on the foam pads and wait until the attendant tells us to. And it's a straight shot. The water instantly cools my skin from the burning sun overhead. My stomach slides up into my chest, but I get used to it, riding the slide until the end. The girls are waiting for us near the exit.

"How was it?" Naima asks, her doe-eyes wide as she bites her lip.

"It was fine."

"It was *boring*," she groans, her shoulders slumping before she points to the long tunnel beside us that requires a hike to get to the top. "Let's try that one."

Mt. Everest is better. It has three different ways you can go. Luna and I line up for the long pipe since it seems to be the least extreme. Naima gets the tunnel that drops into a slide and Sam gets the long slide that looks like it goes straight down. We're staggered where Luna goes first with two other people and then once they're down, the rest of us go. The ride is dark with lights in it. I get stuck towards the top of the pipe and have to scoot along but once I do it's a fast shot towards the end of the river. The minute I see the light at the end of the tunnel,

I'm dunked under. Chlorinated water shoots up my nose, and it's not sexy. I look up, and Naima's staring with a concerned look on her face. When I said, I loved water parks, it was back when I was eight, and Mama used to make me wear goggles with a nose piece and ear plugs. I wasn't even tall enough to ride rides like this.

"Are you okay?" she asks, cupping my face and removing water from around my eyes. Her hands are soft and reassuring which makes me smile.

"Much better. How was it for you?"

"It was perfect!!" Naima exclaims while shuffling to the next line. This one, Pipes Peak, more pipes, another huge dunk pool, except this time, we buddy up.

"I don't know if I want to ride this," Luna says.

"Noooo, Luna," Naima whines.

"We need four people," Sam says.

Luna sighs and stares at the series of tunnels. "I don't know. Do you think it'll be scary?"

"I can ride with you if you're scared," Naima offers.

Sam and I look at each other when we realize that means we'd have to ride together.

"I'll ride with you Luna," Sam's quick to offer.

We let them go first since Luna's liable to leave Sam hanging. They're settling into one pipe and we get into an adjacent one. Luna in front of Sam and Naima in front of me. The attendant lets them go first, and we hear Luna wailing. Naima sucks in air at the sound of it and then we're cleared to go. We're shot into a dark tunnel with glowing lights inside. The roar of water fills our ears, and we're slipping and sliding towards the bottom. I swear it's going at least one hundred miles per hour. It's intense and then blinding light ends it, and we float (thank God) on top of the pool. When I try to get out though, I fall in and more water rushes into my nose.

"That was cute," Naima says. When we reach Sam and Luna, she says, "We can do another Pipes Peak tunnel, but I really want to do Cyclone and then we're done with the tunnels."

We return to the line, but this time we get into the blue tunnel, and similar to the last, we rush through a tunnel until we get into a wide open bowl. We circle around it enjoying the sun on our skin, and the water which has calmed down until the float turns around, and we're rushing through the tunnel backwards. I grab the handles wanting to scream but not in front of Naima.

My heart is racing when we get out of the pool. I'm struggling to catch my breath, and Naima shakes her arms and legs to get the water off. Poor Luna's shivering like she's been left out in the freezing rain.

"I'm *done* with the rides," Luna declares.

"Luna, noooo," Naima cries. "One more and then we can do whatever you want." She presses her hands together praying for Luna to listen.

Luna eventually acquiesces. Naima grabs her hand and interlaces their fingers. Probably so Luna won't run away. We walk past the wave pool. In the distance I see more pools and cabanas. Passing two kid's play areas, we end up back at the attraction at the beginning of the park. It's another buddy ride, and as we climb up the steps to the entrance of the tunnel, I watch the couples slide up the slope higher and higher and then fall down. Everybody's screaming for their life. My heart beats louder, and my stomach sinks lower with each step we take.

"May-maybe I'll sit this one out," I say.

"Nooo," Naima pleads.

"Nah, it's fine. I'm sure Luna wants to take a break, right?" I turn to her, and she looks relieved.

"I'd love to." Her face is apologetic as she turns to Naima who's pouting.

"Hey, it's fine," Sam says. "It's just me and you."

Naima looks from him to Luna and me and then sighs. They place the tube down and get into it. Sam in the front. Naima in the back. Her foot touches his waist, and when she giggles, I feel sick. They go down the shoot, and I catch them on the other side. Naima waves her hands in the air, and with her head tossed back, she screams. Wild and free. Luna and I carry our unused tube back down the stairs and find Naima and Sam walking back to the entrance.

"We're gonna go again. Y'all don't have to wait for us," she explains and grabs our tube.

She's bouncing on the steps as her and Sam talk animatedly about something. It's like when she got her license, and they looked like they were in their own world with me outside of it.

They're just friends, I remind myself. They've been friends longer than I've known all of them combined. That kind of friendship is bound to have a certain level of closeness. Look at her and Luna. They act like a married couple. I'm probably overreacting. That's all.

Luna and I grab tubes for the lazy river. After about twenty minutes, Naima waves at us at the entrance. I stand to help her on her tube so she can get in. Luna floats away in the process so Naima holds onto my hand to stay with me. The lazy river is kinda crowded so if she drifts away, it won't be hard to catch up.

"Where's your friend?" I ask, realizing she came alone.

"Sam? He's in the wave pool. The last time we were in a wave pool together, I almost drowned and he laughed at me." Her eyes widen and her mouth gapes open. "I mean...he made sure I didn't drown, but he laughed at me afterwards. Can you believe him? He's the worst." She shakes her head but grins.

My heart beats furiously in my chest because why does she smile just thinking about him? Why do they have all these little moments between the two of them? Why do they—

"Are you okay?" Naima asks. Her eyebrows knit together in consternation.

"What? No? I'm—I'm fine." I'm overreacting. They're just friends. Naima is my girlfriend. *Mine*. Sam's with Dixie. I was so angry about Ricky touching her that I think every boy is after her. I'm tripping.

"Okay." She rubs her thumb over my knuckles. Her eyes scan my face, assessing, but she drops it.

We stay that way, silently holding hands while our tubes lazily travel around the river. Eventually, we catch up with Luna and float around watching kids play on their water tower, people shoot onto the Backsplash ride, and flowers blossom on the magnolia trees. The cool water on my legs and feet helps me forget about the sun overhead so I chill and tune into the park's early 2000s music playlist. There's times where Naima knows the words so she'll sing along to them under her breath, nodding her head to the beat. We're otherwise silent, taking in this beautiful day, beautiful weather and enjoying each other's company. After our tenth loop around the lazy river, Luna stands to get out. Naima and I keep floating until Luna returns with bottles of water in her hands.

We get out, guzzling the water down, and walk around looking for Sam. We find him in one of the pools tucked away behind the cabanas. It's some of the coldest water in the park which is appreciated because the day's only gotten hotter. I float on the water, letting the water fill my ears and rock my body. The sun's heat only touches my face now. I breathe in and out, and when I look over, Luna's doing the same. Her eyes are closed while she's floating. Her hair spreads out on the water's surface. I can't see Naima when I turn my head, but I can hear her squeal. Of course, her and Sam are playing around in the water together. When she sees that I'm up, she giggles, using her hand to squirt water in my direction. I smile chasing after her and when I catch her, I hold her in my arms and kiss her neck. She giggles, looping her arms around my shoulder. I bring her closer to me, savoring the fact that I can do this and hopefully will be able to for as long as I want.

It's Luna who breaks us up asking if we're hungry.

"I could eat," I shrug.

"Are you thinking about park food?" Naima asks.

"I'm thinking Huddle House," she says and right when she does my stomach growls. It agrees.

Naima pouts.

"We're not staying in the park all day. Let's go change," Luna says.

At the lockers, we're a few shades darker. The girls go to the bathroom to get out of their swimsuits. Sam and I just put our shirts back on. At the Jeep, Luna beats me to the front seat so I sit in the back with Naima. She lays her head on my shoulder, and I wrap my arm around her for the short drive to Huddle House. Walking into Huddle House, it looks like an average American diner except to the far right there's a couple smoking with fans overhead. A small sign next to them says, "Smoking Section." I thought people stopped smoking indoors back in the 1900s, but I guess not.

We sit in a booth that's equidistant from the smoking section and the bathroom. Naima doesn't seem too bothered by the smell of either so I think it's fine. The menu is reminiscent of Waffle House but with more options.

"Whatcha thinking?" Naima asks, leaning over to look at my menu.

It's three in the afternoon so I say, "The burger looks good."

She hums an affirmation and returns to her menu. "Does anyone want eggs?"

For the most part, she doesn't eat eggs, seafood, okra, or nuts. The exception being boiled eggs, fried okra, or nut butter because those have different textures.

"I'll take your eggs," Luna offers.

"Over-easy?" Naima asks and Luna confirms.

"Hey," Sam reaches his arm diagonally on the table to get Naima's attention. "I'm so hungry my front's touching my back."

He grins as she throws her head back laughing. She clutches her chest like it's a joke, but it's not *that* funny.

"You remember that?" he asks.

"Yeah," she nods, then leans over to me to explain. "My dad used to say that all the time when he was starving, and I thought it was the funniest thing I ever heard. He was so country."

I bite my tongue. Of course, Sam's rubbing it in that not

only did he get to meet Naima's dad, but he has fond memories of him too. Her father's another memory that only they share.

The waitress interrupts us and puts their private bonding moment to an end.

"Is it okay if we put in our food orders?" Luna asks, and the waitress nods.

"Together or separate," she asks.

"We're together," I say, pointing from me to Naima.

"Separate," Luna says at the same time Sam says, "Together."

"I got you," he tells Luna, nudging her arm with his elbow. Then he tells the waitress, "We're together too."

Luna looks him up and down then grins. "Maybe I should order more food."

He rolls his eyes at her. "Just order."

Maybe I'm wrong about Sam. Maybe he's that way with all his friends, and I'm just being paranoid because if I fail at getting a job this summer, Naima and I could break up. She could end up with somebody else...somebody like him. We order our food then sit back and wait for it. Sam and Luna immediately pull out their phones and scroll. Naima is sitting beside me, unnaturally still. When I look over, she's hunched over shivering.

"What's wrong?"

"I'm fine," she rushes to say. She looks over her shoulder to the booth behind us and then back at the table.

I reach for her hand to comfort her, but she pulls it away.

"Sorry," she whispers. "It's my hair. It's heavy and wet and it's touching my back and it's—" She shivers again then glances at the empty booth. "Do you think they'll say something if I put my braids over the seat?"

"If they say something, I'll take care of it," I reassure her and she smiles, whipping her braids over the back. They're holding so much water that they smack the vinyl backing of the booth. Her back and shoulders instantly straighten like this huge weight has been lifted off of her. Accommodations can really be that small and simple.

Something pops up on Luna's phone that causes her jaw to tighten and her eyebrows to knit together. She looks up from her phone and right at me. It's Ricky. We don't say anything to each other, but Luna says, "Es curioso que ella no está aquí."

"¿Quién?" Naima asks.

Luna tips her head towards Sam who's absorbed in his phone. She's changing the subject to Dixie. I don't understand what their problem is with her. She seems okay. A little self-obsessed, but we're teenagers. Isn't this the time to be self-absorbed?

Naima sighs and glances towards Sam. Pity crosses her face. "Pienso que...ella usa...a él."

Luna's grimace corresponds with my translation that that may not be the right verb, but I get what she's saying. She thinks Dixie is using Sam.

"Él entiende," Naima says before Luna has a chance to respond. I think about what Sam knows when I realize she's talking about me. That I understand what they're saying.

"Sí, pero *él* no dirá nada," Luna stares at me. The double entendre is clear so I raise my hands to show her I'm not saying anything.

"Es mi querido," Naima says, cupping my jaw and rubbing her thumb over my cheek. Her thumb lands at the corner of my mouth. Her gaze dips to my lips then back up to me. She smiles, and I swear to God my heart stops beating. This is nirvana.

"Biscuits and gravy?" the waitress asks, dragging us back into this world. Luna reaches for the plate, and the waitress passes out the rest of our food. "Let me know if you need anything else."

We dig in. Naima passes the eggs to Luna, and Luna stares at Naima's waffle.

"I should've got that."

"Want a bite?" Naima asks, already cutting her waffle. Luna nods, and Naima offers the fork with the waffle across the table to Luna's mouth. Luna bites it then moans.

"You can have half if you want," Naima says.

"I can't take your waffle. Maybe a fourth," Luna pinches her index finger and thumb.

Naima laughs and cuts a fourth of a waffle for her friend because she loves us, and we love her.

Chapter Sixteen

Kamron

"One time for the birthday boy!" Naima cheers when I open the door for her. She lifts a covered bowl to her head and smiles.

"It's birthday *man*," I say, wrapping my arms around her waist to bring her closer to me.

"Man, huh?" she grins. Her eyes dart over my face then she laughs. "I'm eighteen, and I definitely don't feel like a *woman*. If anything, I'm a glorified child."

"Well, *I'm* a man now."

"Okay, Big Man." She pushes the bowl gently against my chest. "There's your banana pudding. Happy birthday."

My brain short circuits when I hear banana pudding. I grab the bowl and head to the kitchen looking for a spoon when I remember to kiss Naima on the cheek and another on her lip for good measure.

"Thank you," I say. She hums while I grab a spoon and dig

in.

The first bite is euphoric. The pudding is cold and creamy. The bananas are fresh. The cookies have the tiniest amount of crunch to them. I love them when they're soft so it's almost there.

"Is it good?"

I look up from the bowl to see Naima leaning against the entrance to the kitchen.

"You want some?" I offer.

She shakes her head. "Banana pudding is good for exactly two seconds and then it's gross." Her face scrunches up like she's smelled something bad.

I know she made this just for me, but I still want to share the experience with her. I scoop a tiny amount into a spoon and stick it out for her taste.

"Try it. Please," I smile. I'm not above begging.

She hesitantly looks from me to the spoon. "It's for you. I don't think—"

"Can I make it a birthday wish?" I bargain.

She rolls her eyes and then exhales. Tentatively she moves toward the spoon and eats the pudding.

"It's alright. I—" she gags and I panic. Did I push her too far?

She faces her palm out towards me trying to swallow and talk. "The banana is really mushy."

"I thought it was fine." It didn't taste too offensive to me so

I thought she'd be okay.

"Like I said," she repeated. "Banana pudding is good for two seconds—when the bananas are firm and the cookies are hard. Otherwise, it's the grossest shit in existence."

I spoon another bite of pudding in my mouth before setting the bowl on the counter. "I'm sorry. I just wanted you to taste how good it is. I wasn't trying to hurt you." I wrap my arms around her and stare into her eyes so she understands how serious I am.

"There are other ways you can show your appreciation." She taps her finger to my chest then her eyes gaze up at mine before darting all over my face.

Tipping her chin and lips towards mine, my face can't help but to break out into a grin. When her breath reaches my lips, I close the small amount of space between us, kissing her, pulling her closer to me. The sweet smell of her mixes with the banana pudding on our tongues, and I can't stop. My hands reach into her braids. The other digs into her hip, pulling her as close to me as possible. I only stop because I have to breathe. Annoying air.

Before I can go in for another kiss, Naima presses her thumb to my lips.

"I was thinking of *another* way you can appreciate me," she whispers.

I'm about to warn her when Amaya emerges from her bedroom. Naima jumps when she hears her.

"Hey Amaya. Naima's here," I say releasing Naima from the wall I've pinned her to before Amaya says anything I don't need Naima hearing, like how my job search is going or whether or not I'm moving back to California.

"Niece!" she exclaims with her arms wide for a hug. I love how Amaya so quickly accepted Naima into our family and made her feel like she belongs. She does belong. I hope she sees that.

"Hey Amaya," Naima says, sheepishly hugging her. She's probably embarrassed that I didn't warn her about Amaya being here sooner.

"I'm almost done with my lunch break then I'll be outta y'all's hair," Amaya says walking towards the fridge. She looks at the counter. "Is that to share?"

"It's my present," I say, at the same time Naima says, "If you want."

Amaya listens to her, grabbing a fresh spoon to dip into *my* banana pudding then she moans. I stare wide-eyed at Amaya, and Naima giggles, placing her hand on my arm. "You can share, and I can make you some more whenever," she whispers to me.

"But it's my birthday," I mumble.

Amaya swallows. "How was your doctor's appointment by the way?"

Talk about the things we aren't supposed to say in front of Naima. When I glance at Naima, her doe-eyes are wide waiting for my answer.

"It was fine," I say brusquely. The doctor ordered some labs, but other than that, I'm fine. I don't know why Mama didn't wait until I was back in California, but if I don't go back when would I have gone?

When Amaya realizes what she's asked and the implications of it, a silent apology crosses her face before she turns to put the banana pudding in the fridge. I glance at Naima, but I don't think she caught on. Instead we go to my bedroom to get some alone time while Amaya finishes up her lunch break.

The Giants game is still streaming on my laptop. They're up by a run. I sit on the bed and watch our bullpen pitcher throw a strikeout. I pump my fist in the air. The bases are loaded. One more out, and we're out of this messy inning.

Naima groans when she sits on the bed and sees what I'm watching. "First Sam started with his baseball obsession and then Markese, now you. I've worked so hard to avoid having to learn baseball, but it's inescapable."

I mute the laptop and place it on my side table.

"We don't have to listen to the game. What do you want to do?" I ask.

Her eyes travel my body, and she grins.

"Amaya," I whisper.

"Fine." She lays on my pillow and looks up at me. I lean back so she can see the laptop screen.

"What are you reading?"

I follow her gaze to my books that are holding up the laptop. It's *Kindred* by Octavia Butler, *Salvage the Bones* by Jesmyn Ward, *Long Division* by Kiese Laymon, and *We Deserve Monuments* by Jas Hammonds. I tell her exactly that and what each book is about. So far this summer I've read all of them except for *Long Division*. Maybe I'm a masochist, but I've been reading a lot of fiction about the South and the complicated feelings of the people who live here. The mix of pride and fear. The beauty and horror. But so far living here, I've mainly seen the pride and beauty of Mississippi. Maybe it's because I came in here with the worst ideas of the state, and it's proven me wrong in the best of ways. A state that can make someone as caring, compassionate, and curious as Naima can't be all that bad.

Naima's mouth quirks in amusement.

"What?" I ask.

"Do you wear your nerd glasses when you read?" she asks.

I chuckle, shaking my head and reaching over my side table for my glasses, putting them on. I used to have round glasses, but Naima said only slutty boys wear round glasses, and after Naima called me a slut no less than a dozen times, I updated to rectangular frames.

She surprises me by sitting in my lap and kissing me along my jaw. As good as it feels, I'm not super comfortable doing anything with Amaya in the house.

"Naima," I beg.

She hums and redirects her kisses to my neck. She's playing a dangerous game.

"Ama—" I'm cut off by the front door opening.

Naima stops, waiting for Amaya's car door to open, for it to start, and then for her to drive down the road. Her legs wrap tighter around my waist, and I'm embarrassed at how quickly my shorts tighten. She notices immediately, breaking the kiss, looking down at my lap, and then back up to me, grinning. With one hand, I grab her thigh and the other, I hold her neck to flip her over on the bed. She whoops but settles under me, leaning her head to the side for me to kiss her neck. Of course, I oblige. Our fingers interlaced, our hands pinned to the bed. With each kiss on her neck, her hips grind into mine until I can't take it anymore. I slide her dress up. She tugs at my shirt. We undress, and I lean over towards the side table for a condom.

❧

I can't keep having sex with Naima.

She's in my bed napping while I've been making cylinders. It gives me plenty of time to think about the terrible boyfriend I am by not being honest with her. It's not fair to keep having sex with her like everything is okay when it's not, but the only thing I want to do is love her and be with her forever. I'm not lying about the love part, just the forever.

The clay breaks without me trying so I give up. Wiping my hands on a rag, I decide I'll clean the mess later. I sit in my nook and grab my phone. Mama texted a picture of petit fours from Ettore's in the group chat when she texted happy birthday. She knows they're my favorite. She's been sending pics of my favorite Sacramento things to entice me to come back quicker, but desserts aren't enough to make me give up Naima. She's the best thing about Mississippi.

Jada texts asking what I'm doing. I think about video calling her, but I don't want Naima to overhear. Walking out of the studio, I check my room, and she's still napping. The scarf she leaves here is sliding around her braids, and her mouth is gaped open with her soft snores. She looks peaceful, beautiful, content. I sigh. I want her to stay that way as long as possible.

Walking out the back door into the hot humid air, I call Jada and sit on a bench. She answers standing in her bathroom while she's getting ready. I remember it's a little after eleven there.

"Happy birthday baby brother," she says, blending some product into her face.

"Where you getting all dressed up and going?" I ask her.

She raises her eyebrows and tilts her head towards the phone. "I'm an adult."

"I'm just asking," I laugh.

"If you must know," —she looks in her mirror instead of at the phone— "I'm going out with London and Aaliyah. Do you remember Carter? White mama? Green eyes? Aaliyah's dating him now." She shakes her head disapprovingly.

Carter's younger brother, Caleb, and I played Little League together. Carter was six years older than us so he'd drop Caleb off at games sometimes, usually with a different girl in his car. I used to think he was badass, and somebody I wanted to grow up and be. I'm glad I grew out of that.

"What you got against Carter?" I ask.

"He's a hoe."

Jada places her hands on the sink and laughs. I laugh with her, and it's cleansing. Finally, she picks the brush back up and asks, "So how you've been? Taking care of yourself?"

"Trying to," I say.

"How's Naima?"

"She's in my bed. Asleep."

Jada sits down and angles the phone at her face so she can look directly at me. "Have you figured out your situation?"

I exhale. Have I? I decide to share the good news. "Well, I've gotten one interview so far."

"What? That's amazing!"

I got the call yesterday afternoon. It sucked that I couldn't schedule the interview today after my doctor appointment while I was already in Jackson, but I'll drive back down in two weeks for my interview. "I hope this works out because I think the other jobs ghosted me."

"They do that," Jada says, applying mascara. "So do you

think you'll get it? Do you think you're staying?"

"I hope so." Staying means I don't have to feel guilty for enjoying my time with Naima.

Jada turns to the screen. Her lips thin into a line. "Well Pops is watching the Giants games for the first time in years, and Mama's had your room cleaned. Twice."

She's leaving the quiet part unsaid: that they're both preparing for me to be home again. I haven't been home since last summer when I visited for two weeks and told my parents I wanted to stay in Mississippi for another year. Pops took it better than Mama. Neither took it well. I spent the entire two weeks there video calling Naima and telling her how much I missed her. But I got to spend another year with Naima. I'm grateful for it, but I wish it wasn't passing by so quickly.

"I'll stop by sometime this summer," I promise.

Jada's smile is bittersweet. "Well, I'm glad you called. I get to say happy birthday in person," she shrugs. "As close to in person as we can get."

"It was good seeing you," I say and I mean it. As much as I love being here, I think I'll always miss home and her.

"Take care, baby brother. Tell Naima I asked about her. Love you," she says.

"Love you too." I gently lift the corner of my lips. Her face disappears leaving the black screen. I rest my elbows on my thighs and hold my head in my hands.

Fifty-three days until Naima starts college.

Chapter Seventeen

Kamron

We're watching *Everything Everywhere All At Once* at Sam's house. We decided on a movie night when she was at my house a few days ago for my birthday. It's Naima's favorite movie about an Asian family navigating family trauma throughout multiple universes. Sam, Luna, and Eric are here too. It's my first time meeting Eric even though he's been with Naima's family for the past month and a half. He's shorter. Probably around 5'6. Dark skin, round face, and a shaved head.

Sam's in the kitchen, and Naima's leaning over the island with her full attention on him so I walk over there, wrapping my arm around her waist.

"What's up?" I ask.

"He makes the best popcorn, and he won't tell me what's in it. Have you had it?" She turns her back to the kitchen island to face me.

"No."

"Well it's addictive. It's like salty, but really sweet, and I know it has caramel, chocolate chips, and salt, maybe butter, but he won't tell me what else." She twists her face at him.

"It's a secret," he says, stirring something brown and sticky in a pot.

"I can keep a secret!" she argues with him.

He lifts an eyebrow. "Sure, Nai."

He turns off the eye for the brown syrup before grabbing a wide skillet and setting that on the stove and turning it on. He pours oil into the pan and waits for it to heat by hovering his palm above it.

"Are you making the spicy popcorn again?" Naima asks.

"What's this I hear about spicy popcorn?" Eric asks, coming up on the other side of me.

"I cook it in chili oil," Sam explains.

"Oh, so you can tell him your secrets but not me?"

Sam grins with his back to her, still focusing on heating the oil. This is their game I guess, the back and forth playful teasing.

"We haven't met," Eric says, with his hand out. "I'm Eric."

"Kamron," I say, shaking his hand.

"I've heard so much about you," Eric says, nodding to Naima. "Extremely pretty."

I laugh. Of course that's how Naima would describe me. No one's ever called me pretty before she did. Handsome, attractive, cute, maybe, but pretty makes me feel dainty and precious and shit.

"I'm sure I'm more than just a pretty face to her," I say to Eric but grin at Naima.

"That's literally the first thing she said when she saw you," Luna chimes in, and my mouth gapes open.

"And here I was thinking you hated me. 'Annoying' is the word you used."

It was "él me molesta" specifically. It hurt that this girl I thought so much about thought so little of me, but she apologized the next day, and now knowing that she was already impressed with me makes me feel silly that I tried so hard to impress her. Naima winces from the memory of her calling me annoying.

"Oh my gosh, you're never gonna let that go, are you?" She hangs her head back, exasperated.

"Nah. It hurt my feelings." I pout, placing my hands over my injured heart.

"I have more than made up for it." Her eyes travel up and down my body, a grin tugging her lips.

I bite my lower lip, lean towards hers, and whisper, "You can make up for it a little bit more."

As I kiss her, a pillow hits my side.

"Ow!" I react, turning in the direction of its thrower: Luna.

"Quit being gross, you two."

Naima giggles and kisses me again on the cheek. While we

were talking, Sam popped a batch of popcorn on the stove. He spread the popcorn on a sheet pan lined with parchment and then poured the brown syrup over it. Naima's eyes follow the syrup as it drizzles over.

"You are not eating all the popcorn again." Luna taps Naima's shoulder.

"You have to make me my own batch." Naima leans over the counter to tell Sam.

"I will. Don't worry," he says, saving some of the syrup in the pot.

It takes him another fifteen minutes to finish making Naima her popcorn and the spicy popcorn. I'm not gonna lie, the spicy popcorn is pretty good. Better than I thought it would be. It's crunchy, salty and there's a slight tingle in your mouth from the chili oil. It's very addictive.

Sitting around the living room, Sam and I are on opposite sides in armchairs while Luna, Naima, and Eric squeeze together on the couch sharing an oversized blanket. I haven't seen *Everything Everywhere All At Once* since it came out a couple of years ago, but knowing all the plot twists, I see them unraveling from the very beginning. Waymond doing parkour on the security feeds. The bagel symbol on the receipt. The parallels between Joy and Jobu. It's all there front and center. Innocuous at first, but impossible to unsee once you've seen it.

I settle into the movie as it takes me on a roller coaster of emotions: laughter, disgust, anger, sadness, and love. There's never a dull moment in this movie, and I'm starting to see why Naima loves it so much. Although there's so much to appreciate the first time around, we have to watch it again and again to really see the nuances and intricacies. Damn, is this gonna be one of my favorite movies too?

I'm glued to the screen when Evelyn gives into her despair. She's sabotaging her entire life because Jobu has convinced her that nothing is worth living for. Nihilism is better than belief. In each universe, she pushes away the people that believe in her and walk towards the bagel, but she looks back for Waymond. In the superstar universe where her and Waymond are independently successful and separated from each other, Waymond tells her that he's not naive for being kind. Kindness is strategic and necessary. Before he leaves her, he shares his final words about how he would've loved a simple life just doing laundry and taxes together. It's been memed to death, but it's a beautiful notion. That love is simply wanting to spend time with someone else. No ulterior motives. No conditions. No struggle between the two of you. Just love.

"You're crying again, Nai?" Sam groans.

I shift my attention to Naima whose nose and cheeks have turned the darkest pink her brown skin will allow. She sniffles and dots her nose with the blanket. How did I miss that?

"Shut up, Sam."

She turns towards Luna and interlaces their fingers. While

staring at their hands, she says, "It's just that love is doing something so mundane with someone and being so happy that they're there with you and...and," she sniffles, and Luna wraps her arm around her.

"I know," she whispers into Naima's shoulder.

In less than three weeks, Luna and her family leave for Mexico. I already know it's gonna break Naima which is why I'm trying so hard to stay for her. I have to ace this interview.

Sam pauses the movie and stares at the two of them holding each other tight on the couch. His jaw clenches but his eyes—it's that same look that I saw at the baseball game, by his Jeep, and at the water park. At first I couldn't place it, but now it's undeniable. I know that look. Intimately.

He's in love with her.

I stare from him looking at Naima to Naima staring at Luna. Both with eyes full of love so thick and obvious that anyone could see it. But Naima is so forthright and giving of her love and Sam hides it.

Because of me.

The realization sits heavy on my chest. If I wasn't here, would Naima be with Sam? Am I the only thing stopping them from being together? If I leave, is she going to be with him? Will he replace me? Will she forget I ever existed? Will she remember the way I love her, the way I hold her?

I'm replaceable.

Yeah, if I leave, she's going to forget everything I'm trying so hard to make her remember. Tears fill my eyes, but I clear my throat and push them away.

When I look up, Naima's staring at me, her wide eyes puffy and pink. Eric gets up and walks toward me, and I take his seat beside her and hold her. Her free hand reaches for mine and squeezes it.

"You okay?" I ask, and she nods, kissing my cheek, before laying her head on my shoulder. She wants *me*. I have to remember this. When we're both spiraling, we reach for the other to ground us.

"Y'all ready to keep watching?" Sam asks with the remote in his hand.

Naima looks from me to Luna then nods. "Yeah. We're ready."

Chapter Eighteen

Naima

NAIMA: Are you busy Saturday?

LUNA: No, why?

Eric wants to take us out

To a club

With his friends

Are they cute?

Pretty sure they're gay.

But are you free?

I don't know. I've never been to a club. Will it be safe?

Me either and idk

We only have 11 days until you leave

Are you really counting down the days?

You know I am.

Once we get to the single digits, I'm gonna cry every day.

Be prepared

Naima you cry if a leaf falls

Ik. It's so beautiful.

You cry when you run out of capri suns

You cry when it rains

It's the perfect time to cry.

And you haven't answered my question?? Are you coming with us???

I guess I can come

Yay! We're gonna have fun!

Also you're worth every tear I cry because I love you

Chapter Nineteen

Naima

Mom rented an apartment for us in Fondren, the artsy neighborhood in Jackson. Eric gave us the bare minimum information about where we're going probably because he was scared we wouldn't come. Luna is in a red halter crop top and a black mini skirt, and she let me borrow her navy blue bodycon mini dress. Eric drives us to an unassuming building. It may have been a grocery store in its old life, but its windows are now blocked out in rainbow colors and the bass thumps from inside.

There's a bouncer at the door who checks us for weapons before we can walk in and meet a man who checks our IDs. He gives us Under 21 bracelets then lets us in. Smoke perfumes the air, thick and heavy over the central bar. To our left, there's two pool tables with overhead lights. The music vibrates from a room past the bar where blue, purple, and green lights dance across the floor.

Eric waves to some friends and leads us over to them. Kai is Asian and wears a silver mesh top over their abs with loose black cargo pants. Damson is Black and has on a loose green short sleeved button up and matching shorts. Both hug Eric when they reach each other.

"Is this a gay club?" Luna whispers to me.

"I think so," I whisper back.

Kai and Damson reach out to hug us too.

"Come dance with us," Damson says.

Kai grabs my hand, and Damson grabs Luna's. They didn't have to ask me twice. The DJ plays house music, and Kai takes my hand, twirling me around. I swing my hips along to the beat. Okay maybe not their beat, but it's definitely to a beat. They laugh and pull me close to them. Their arm's on mid back as my legs interlock with theirs. A bit of breathing room lies between us as we dance together on the beat. Our bodies move in a way that's cathartic. Although we just met and we're dancing close, there's a certain level of respect and trust that we build.

"You want a drink?" they whisper in my ear, breathless once the music transitions to something a little less high-energy.

"No. I'm eighteen." I raise my wrist to show the bracelet.

"They don't care," they smirk.

"Are y'all getting a drink?" Luna detaches from Damson. "I want one."

"What do you want?" Kai asks.

"Surprise me," Luna says, and Kai leaves with Damson for the bar.

I spin around the dance floor looking for Eric, and he's in the corner of the room pinned up against the wall with some man twice his size hovering over him. He's smiling so I take that as a sign he likes it there.

"Do you want to walk around?" I ask Luna, tugging my dress down. She takes my hand and taps Damson's shoulder when we pass them at the bar waiting for drinks.

We walk past a locked closed door on the way to the pool table. Both pool tables are full with people playing. I've never played, but I want to so we lean against the wall and watch the teams laugh, drink, and hit the balls. When one of the teams finishes, two people walk away and the other two rerack the balls.

"You wanna play?" the Hispanic woman asks us.

I look at Luna at the same time she looks at me.

"We don't know how to play," Luna says, hesitantly walking towards the table.

The woman hands her a pool stick. "Neither do we. I'm Patricia by the way."

"Luna. This is Naima."

"Rachel." The Black woman she's with raises her hand while still looking at her phone.

The two of them look like older versions of us. Black and Hispanic except Patricia is taller than Luna. Her hair is in a low ponytail, and she's wearing a black button down with the sleeves rolled up mid-arm. Her shirt is tucked into her high waisted jeans. And Rachel is tiny—both in size and height. She may only be five feet with her high heels on.

"This your first time at WonderLust?" Patricia asks.

So that's the name of this place.

"Yeah," I finally speak to her. "We're with my cousin, Eric."

"Cool, cool." She rubs the tip of her pool stick into the chalk. "This is Rachel's first time."

"I have a girlfriend," Rachel shares, probably trying to dissuade us from hitting on her.

"Yeah. I have a boyfriend, but Luna here is single." I widen my hands to show her off like the prize she is.

Junior year Luna had a brief fling with a girl. I know she keeps trying to pretend it didn't happen, but we're eighteen now. We're high school graduates, and we don't have to be what everyone else wanted us to be while we were in high school. We can reinvent ourselves or fully discover parts of ourselves that we've previously had to hide to survive.

Luna widens her eyes at me and mumbles at me to shut up, but Patricia lifts her eye and smirks.

"I'm moving in less than two weeks. I'm just here to have fun."

"We can have fun," Patricia grins. "Where you moving to?"

"Back to Mexico."

"Ah. ¿Hablas español?"

"Sí. Soy mexicaña."

"Okay. Soy boricua."

"Yo también."

I look back and forth between them grinning. Patricia gives Luna a once-over, and I want to squeal. Even I can see what's going on between them.

"You wanna break?" Patricia asks.

Luna closes the gap between them and angles her body perpendicular to Patricia's. The white ball barely touches the rest of them, but I fear she did better than I would have. Patricia follows up afterwards and actually hits several balls, knocking a solid ball in the hole.

"You're stripes. We're solids," she says.

"So I hit the striped balls?" I ask clarifying because this is the first time I've ever played, and I want to avoid further embarrassment by hitting the wrong ball.

She nods. As I'm trying to see which ball I can hit, Kai finally shows up with Luna's drink.

"It's a tequila sour," they tell her, handing her the drink and then returning to the smoky, black ether of the club.

I hit the white ball, and it hits a few balls. I know a striped one is in there. Rachel sits her phone down for the first time since we've started talking to them, but she doesn't make contact with any other ball. She picks her phone back up and ignores us.

Patricia seems like she's the only one who knows what she's

doing which is whooping our asses. On her turn, she's sliding the stick back and forth in the crevice between her thumb and index finger. She hits another solid ball in and walks around the table looking for her next hit.

"Are y'all staying for the drag show?" she asks.

Drag show? The excitement is apparent on both Luna and my faces.

"First time, too?" Patricia laughs. "I guess it's a first time for everything."

She hits a solid ball, and it moves but doesn't go in. My turn. As I get ready to hit a striped, Patricia continues, "The doors open in about twenty minutes if y'all wanna go in. We can sit together."

She points to the locked door we passed, and we nod.

After Patricia almost single handedly wins the game, we stand around the table talking until the doors open. The room is cozy. There's tables on either side of an aisle leading to a lit stage. Patricia was right. The area fills up fast. People shuffle in and grab the seats or start reserving seats for their friends. There's a table in the middle of the room we're able to snag. Patricia opens her arms to let us in first. I sit, then Luna, Patricia, and Rachel. The show doesn't start for another thirty minutes so I look around for Eric. He's not seated. I haven't seen him since we saw him talking to that guy in the dance room. There's people standing around the room, but I don't see him, Kai, or Damson. I text him to ask where he's at and hope he's okay.

Patricia asks us where we're from, and Luna answers, "Redbud Springs. It's a small town about an hour and a half north of here."

"Cool, cool," Patricia nods. "I'm from Galveston."

"Texas?" I ask.

"Yeah," she says. "We go to Jackson State. I'm a junior—well about to be a junior and Rachel's a senior. We're roommates."

"You're in college?" I ask, wondering which of my many questions can I ask her without overwhelming her. "What's it like?"

"Uhhh...freedom. The classes are pretty cool and the professors treat you like family. You going?"

"No," I say. "I'm going to Millsaps. It's right up the road."

I thought about going to an HBCU like Dad or a state school like Mom, but when I visited those schools, they were massive and so were the classes. I was afraid of being lost and overwhelmed. I loved the promise of a small tight-knit community and well-rounded education at Millsaps so I decided to go there.

"Yeah. I've heard of it," Patricia says.

An announcement says that the show will start in ten short minutes.

"Do y'all have ones?" Patricia asks.

"No." We both say.

Patricia pulls out a roll and hands us a few. "You give it to the performers you like. The better the performance, the more money you give them."

Anticipation buzzes in the air, and my toes tap against the paved floor while I wait for the show to start. After another announcement, a large white drag queen walks onstage in a tall red wig and black leotard. She shares the rules of the show and ends with, "The use of flash photography is strictly mandatory."

We cheer, and the first performer comes out to a Lady Gaga ballad. She stands center stage. Her blonde hair is in majestic curls, and she's wearing a long blue sequined gown. After the first chorus, the beat changes into something more uptempo, and she rips off the bottom part of the gown to reveal a leotard. The crowd cheers. She dances along to the music, aggressively lip-syncing every word of the song. She stops at each aisle to grab dollar bills, shaking her hips until she gets to the back. There she finishes her song twerking on a stranger. I thought it was cute, but I only have two dollars in my hands so I keep them.

The next performer, Ericka Alexandra, comes out in pink high heel boots, a huge afro, and a pink bodysuit tucked into short shorts. "Freak Nasty" by Megan the Stallion comes on, and the performer runs to the end of the runway while rapping about running through a house like a tomb raider. She twerks on participants while lip-syncing the lyrics. When she goes from aisle to aisle, I stand up to hand her one of my dollar bills because the *Tina Snow* EP is a masterpiece. As she grabs it, she winks, and I realize that Ericka Alexandra is Eric Hudson, my cousin. He's a drag queen.

"Ericka Alexandra" finishes her set by doing a splits on the stage, and the audience goes wild. So he's finding some use from his years as a high school cheerleader.

"That's Eric," I say to Luna whose mouth gapes open.

"What's happening?" Patricia leans over Luna placing her hand on Luna's thigh as she does so.

"That was my cousin," I say, flapping my hands. I can't believe he'd keep something like this secret from me. Wait, is this outing him?

"That's cool," Patricia says, turning her attention back to the show but leaving her hand on Luna's thighs.

I look up at Luna to see if she's seeing what I'm seeing. Of course she's seeing it, she's *feeling* it, but Luna shifts her legs towards Patricia, and Patricia's hand inches up but stays there on her thigh.

After their first performances, the drag queens come out for a second one. For Ericka Alexandra's, she's dancing to a Beyoncé song using choreography from Beyoncé's latest tour. I'm dancing with Erica and give her my dollar when she comes by. Call it nepotism, but Ericka was the best performer. She deserves my little two dollars.

When the show finishes, we follow Patricia past the dance floor outside to a little nook with some benches. Some people are sitting and standing around vaping or smoking. We spot a corner and decide to stand there. I sit on the ground because I'm tired of standing. Looking up at the sky, I can't see the stars like I can at home. The streetlights get in the way of it. Instead I close my eyes, inhale the blends of smells from the tobacco and scented vapor, and listen to the distant ambulance of the city. This will be my home in two short months. I look around at the people of varying sizes, skin colors, gender expressions, and sexual orientations. These could be my people when I move here. Then I look at Luna giggling as Patricia whispers something in ear and sigh. These could be my people without Luna because Luna leaves in eight days.

When she looks from Patricia to me, I smile. I hope she's having fun. I hope when she remembers this day, she'll remember me even when she's miles away in Mexico.

Luna walks towards me and squats in my face. "You doing alright?" she asks and I nod. "I think I'm gonna head out."

I glance around her to Patricia who's waiting for her. "You sure?"

Will she be safe? Patricia is cool, but she's still a stranger, and we're in a big city.

"I'll be fine." Luna places her hand on my knee to reassure me. "I'll text you my location. If anything happens, I'll call you."

"Okay." I bite my lips then grab her hand before she gets up. "Have fun."

She looks at Patricia over her shoulder then back to me. "I will."

My hands in prayer position, I place them to my lips and watch Luna leave with Patricia. I reach into my bra strap and slide out my phone. There's a text from Sam asking us how the club is. I text him that it's a gay bar. I went to a drag show, and Luna went home with a girl. After I send him the text, Luna texts her location, and I breathe a sigh of relief. A baby sigh. I won't be happy until I know she's one hundred percent okay and back in the rental with us.

Sam takes a while to text back, and that's when I check the clock to see that it's almost one in the morning. Way past my bedtime. I stand and see Eric on the dance floor, still in drag. His fans surround him, but he breaks them up when he sees me.

"Can I call you Eric or is that—" I tease.

"—shut up," he cuts me off and rolls his eyes. "I'm still Eric."

"Why didn't you tell me?"

"What's there to tell? I dress up in drag on the weekends to make a little extra money. Your family kicked me out because being gay was okay; drag was pushing it."

"My family?" I ask. I know he's not talking about the same family that disowned me because of how my brain works.

"They wanted me to work at Burger King or something, but here—" He spreads his arms wide. "I feel alive. I feel like me. I can't give that up."

"Are you ready to go?" I ask. I'm glad he's found something that makes him feel alive, but it's bedtime.

"Yeah," he laughs and reaches into his pockets. "But you gotta drive."

⌁

Luna returns around ten the next morning. Her location hadn't changed since last night so I assumed she was either sleeping or dead. I'd been peeking out the blinds and texting Sam and Kamron my worries all morning trying to calm down. They both in different ways told me I was over-reacting. Kamron asked if I could come over later today, but I'll probably spend the rest of the day sleeping the stress away.

Luna walks up the driveway with a smile on her face and a spring in her step. I'm glad she's safe, but she could've at least told me. She swings the front door wide open, sighs happily, and then shuts the door leaning against it with a blissful face.

"Are you okay?" I ask.

"I'm better than okay," she smiles.

"Check out's in less than an hour," Eric walks into the foyer.

"I gotta shower real quick then I'll be ready," Luna says, rushing past me to the room we shared.

I'm already dressed, packed, and my bag's in the car. I pace in the living room biting my lip while Luna hums in the shower and takes her sweet time getting dressed. Eric suggests that we eat at a brunch spot in Fondren so we do. We sit outside on the porch of a cafe. The sun bares itself on my arm so I rub the sting away while keeping my anxiety and frustration at bay. Luna is safe and back with us. That's all that matters.

"So," Eric starts, smearing butter on his biscuit. "How was your night?"

Luna jerks out of her daydream and grins. "Good."

"Good? I saw you leaving last night with that butch and everything was just *good*?"

"Okay it was great," Luna breaks out into a full-blown smile. I've never seen her so happy talking about a date. Usually it's laced with frustration and disappointment, but this time she seems giddy? Luna's almost never giddy.

"We talked all night and then we started making out. One thing led to the other, and," she smiles again, turning her attention to the road next to the cafe. "I'm sorry, Naima."

I look up from my chicken and biscuit. What is she apologizing for?

"I used to think you were lying when you talked about sex feeling right or bragging about Kamron doing it better than everyone else. It made me think that I was doing something wrong cause it just felt like I was there, and the boys felt like they didn't care about me. It felt like I was used and thrown away."

I reach my hand across the table to hold onto hers.

"I know what you mean now when you say that sex should

feel right."

I can't help but to share her smile with her. This is a big moment for her. Yes, I was worried about her being kidnapped and murdered, but she's experiencing the joys of sex with someone who sees her as a valuable participant in it. Sex can be a lot of things. Messy, fun, awkward, beautiful, and loving, but most importantly, it must feel right.

We stare at each other with our fingers interlaced across the table telepathically letting the other know that we see and support her. Eric clears his throat because we've probably made him uncomfortable. Still holding onto Luna's hand, I glare at him but then ask her, "Are you gonna keep talking to Patricia?"

"God, no," Luna shudders. "This is one and done."

"Wait, but what about the feeling right? You two hit it off."

"I'm leaving next week, Naima," she reminds me as if I need the reminder that my best friend is moving to another country.

"Is Mexico accepting of people like us?" Eric asks.

"I've heard some places are," Luna says. "I don't know about Oaxaca, but I don't think anything's as bad as small town Mississippi."

"The United States as a whole isn't as progressive as they claim to be," I mumble to Eric.

"You right about that," he agrees.

"But when we get settled, y'all should come visit," Luna says. "Next summer?"

"I guess we can have The Best Summer Ever, Part Two," I

smile, but it's bittersweet because either way my best friend still leaves me in a week.

Chapter Twenty

Kamron

I have no idea what I just said. I shake the interviewer's hand when we finish, flash her my best smile, and thank her when she says she'll be in touch. Her name's Laurel. She's a short thin white woman. Looks to be in her mid-to-late twenties. Walking back to my car, I try to remember as much about the job as possible. As the office coordinator, I'd be working with Laurel—who's the office manager—as her assistant, emailing clients, managing client portfolios, and working on new policies to make the office more efficient. It seems easy enough plus Laurel said I'd be trained for the job so there's no worries about my lack of experience. It seems like I'm one step closer to making my dreams a reality.

I call Jada through the car once I'm on the interstate back to Redbud Springs. She picks up almost immediately.

"What do I owe this surprise phone call?" Jada asks.

I chuckle. "I just finished my interview."

"And?"

"I think it went well. She seemed really nice and if I get the job, I'd be trained to work under her."

"Do you have any backups in case you don't get the job?"

Backups? With the success of this application and interview, I thought I wouldn't need any backups. July is right around the corner so I really need this to work out, or Pops will make me move back. That was our deal.

"You didn't apply to anything else did you?" Jada asks.

"No. I applied to some other jobs, but this was the only one I heard back from."

I can hear the disapproval in her sigh, but she changes the subject. "I hope you get it. How much are they offering for it?"

"Twelve dollars an hour."

"Hmm," she thinks. "Forty hours is a little under two thousand a month before taxes. How much is rent in Jackson?"

"I don't know," I admit. I never thought past having to get a job.

She's typing away on her phone before she whistles, "Average rent price is ten-fifty. I'm sure Mama and Pops would help with rent."

"Mama said if I stay in Mississippi, they're cutting me off." And with rent being over half of my check, if I budget, I'm sure I'll be okay.

Jada sucks in a breath. "I'll look for some more affordable places then." She's silent on the other side of the call, but a few minutes later she shares, "I found a studio within walking distance of Naima. It's eight hundred dollars."

"That's not too bad, right?" I ask. I admit I have no idea how things work in the real world, but an eight-hundred dollar apartment means I would have more money for food, clay, and other stuff.

"The good news is that rent and utilities are included in that eight hundred. The bad news is that it's the size of a dorm room," Jada says.

"A dorm room isn't that bad," I say, trying to see the bright side. "It's not like I'll be there for long, you know. Just to sleep or if Naima wants to come over, right?"

"So I found another apartment," Jada says, ignoring me. "It's a little further away, but it's bigger: two beds, one bath. It's only eight hundred fifty, but I'd recommend getting a roommate."

"Wait, why?"

"Well Mama and Pops aren't helping you and with you taking home fifteen hundred dollars a month, rent would be over half—"

"Wait, fifteen hundred. What happened to the two thousand dollars?" I ask.

"Taxes," she explains. "If you could split rent would someone, you'd have money for important things like food—"

"How important is food really?" I joke.

Jada sighs. "Kamron, I'm serious. You have to take care of

yourself, especially if you're serious about living alone."

"I know," I say soberly. "This was just a lot more than I thought it'd be."

To be honest, I thought if I got the job, everything else would sort itself out. I'd be able to move to Jackson, keep dating Naima, and when she finishes college, we could get married. I didn't think that this first step of getting a job and then moving to Jackson would have so many obstacles, especially without my parents' help.

"This is real life, baby brother," Jada reminds me.

Up until this point, I've never had to worry about money. My parents gave it to me. I never had to worry about bills or food or how to survive on my own because someone was always there to take care of me, first my parents then Amaya. What am I going to do when it's just me taking care of me? How am I going to survive without any of their help? How can I be there for Naima when it seems like I'm going to struggle to be there for myself?

The questions pester me while driving down the long expanse of I-55. Thick green trees border the highway, and the traffic has thinned out. I exhale wondering how am I going to do this? Am I in over my head? My fingers tap the steering wheel itching to use the wheel.

My wheel! If I'm working forty hours a week and seeing Naima after work and on the weekends, when will I have time to work on my art? Will I have to choose one over the other?

Is it even possible? How can I choose between the two things I love the most?

CHAPTER TWENTY-ONE

Naima

NAIMA: You know how you want me to spend the night tomorrow?

LUNA: Yes?

Well I've been thinking

You're not coming?

Of course I'm coming!

I wouldn't miss it for the world.

So I've been thinking

I'm ready to get a nose piercing with you. It'll be our last hurrah

Kamron said he'd take us

So?

Okay. I'll do it.

Yay!!! It's Piercing Time!

Shut up

Chapter Twenty-Two

Naima

The bright fluorescent light of the tattoo shop pierces my eyes, but I squint and try to power through it. On either side of me is Kamron and Luna, both holding a hand. We've already checked in and are waiting for them to call us.

"Luna?" a burly man with tattooed arms asks, looking at a sticky note. He peers down at us then asks, "Are you both getting piercings?"

I nod while Luna says, "Yes."

"You can come back."

We all follow him to a curtained room where he wipes down a black leather examination table and then motions for Luna to sit on it. He puts on gloves then wipes her nose before asking, "Have you thought about where you wanted to place it?"

We've already talked about this. Luna wants her piercing on her right. I want mine on my left. Once Luna looks in the mirror and points to the place, the man puts a dot on her nose.

He then pulls out this long needle and tells her to close her eyes. Maybe I should've gone first. I know watching it will make it worse for me because I'll know just how terrifying it looks to get the piercing. I grab Kamron's hand, and he squeezes it back before rubbing my shoulder.

"It's okay," he whispers near my ear. "You want me to get one too?"

I turn to him and caress his wide beautiful nose. He'd look even more perfect with a nose piercing.

"Only if you want to," I tell him.

"I want to."

"You're all set," the burly man says. We turn back to Luna and the big scary needle is gone. "You ready?" he asks me.

I gulp and hesitantly walk towards the table. Luna's nose is pink. Her eyes are watering, but she's smiling so I'm happy.

He wipes down the table for me and changes his gloves again before wiping my nose and asking me where I want my piercing. Probably sensing my anxiety, he tells me to close my eyes, and I obey. I try to push the image of the long terrifying needle out of my mind, but that's all I can think of. The long needle going through my face and—*just breathe, Naima*.

"You gotta stay still," the man gently insists.

"Sorry."

"Okay, breathe in," he instructs, and I do. A sharp searing pain juts through my nose, and my eyes instantly water. "All done."

I open my eyes, and there's no long terrifying needle in my eyesight. Only a dull ache on my left nostril. The burly man rubs my arm. "You doing okay?"

I nod. "It wasn't that bad. Thank you."

I check myself out in the mirror with Luna when Kamron asks if he can squeeze in. The man wipes the table again and asks him to find the place he wants. Kamron stands in the mirror with me and Luna and asks us what's a good spot. Grazing his nose, I leave my thumb on his left nostril as well. He looks at me and grins. It takes everything in me not to kiss him right there.

Kamron gets his piercing, and the burly man gives us instructions for cleaning the wound. Kamron pays for all of our piercings before we leave. He wants to sit down and eat at some place before he drops us off at Luna's, but I want to spend as much alone time with Luna as possible before she leaves. Who knows when I'll get to see her again?

At her house, Luna heads for the door, but I hang back to say goodbye to Kamron.

"Thank you for taking us tonight."

"Of course. You want me to pick y'all up tomorrow?"

"Sam's coming. To say goodbye to Luna." Kamron makes some face, probably because he wants to see me again.

"But I can see you the day after, okay?" I compromise. I need the distraction from Luna leaving that morning.

"Okay."

When my thumb caresses his cheek, he says, "I love you."

"I know."

He grabs my fingers and kisses them before pulling me into a kiss. When our noses touch, it jerks the newly pierced stud.

"Ow," we say simultaneously.

"Hey, hey, we can still do this." He kisses my knuckles. "Good night."

I smile at him wishing him a good night.

He waits until I'm in the house before pulling out of the driveway. Mr. and Mrs. Hernandez watch TV in the living room. Thankfully they wave at me instead of wanting a full blown conversation. I walk down the hall to Luna's room where Nellie greets me like she always does.

"Hola, Gatita," I say.

"Do you want her?" Luna asks, sitting on her bed. "We have to give her back to the shelter."

I turn from Luna to the tiny black kitty standing on the floor yelling at me to pick her up. "What? No. Why does she have to go?"

"We won't be able to move with her."

I pick up Nellie and cradle her in my arms. She purrs while I stroke her fur. She's such a tiny perfect baby. I'm sure she'll find another home, but then I remember that people hate cats for simply being black, and she may be overlooked and neglected.

"You know Mom has allergies and doesn't believe pets belong in the house." She doesn't understand how cat equals baby.

"It sucks, but there's nothing we can do. Nobody we know will take her."

I rub Nellie's jaw, and she releases a tiny meow. She's unaware of how her world will change in just a few short days. Holding Nellie, I sit on the bed beside Luna.

"I hate this."

"I hate it too," Luna smooshes her lips together, laying down on the bed.

Setting the kitty on the floor, I lay beside her. Tomorrow Luna and her family pack their belongings to be shipped, and the next day, they get on a plane to Mexico. After eight years of having this funny, creative, beautiful, amazing person in my life, she'll be gone.

"Do you remember when you first came here?" I ask her.

We were in the same fourth grade class. I had never met someone from another country, and I wanted to ask so many questions about life, not only outside of Mississippi, but outside of the United States. She could answer none of them because she didn't speak English.

"I just remember being confused all the time," she laughs. "I remember you being the only person who tried to help me, and you didn't laugh at me when I couldn't say a word right."

"You don't laugh at me when I speak bad Spanish," I say.

"Because you're the only one who's tried to meet me halfway."

My favorite thing about Luna is that we've always understood each other and what it was like to not understand the language of the people around us so we created our own.

"Thank you for that." She turns her head to face me. "Thank you for always making me feel like I'm not alone. Thank you for loving me and being my best friend."

I can't help it. A tear waters my eye. "Thank you for loving *me* and being *my* best friend."

She squeezes my hand. "I hate you. You're gonna make me cry."

I wrap my arm around her. "I've been crying all week."

We hold each other and let the tears clear our sadness away. I wipe her tears away with my thumb and gaze at the pinkness overtaking her honey brown face. Her eyes fill with more tears when she remembers that this is goodbye. Our last sleepover.

"What Little Mix song does this remind you of?" she sniffles.

That's easy.

In a shaky, tear-stained voice, I sing "Between Us." It's the lullaby we fall asleep to.

When I wake up the next morning, Sam is already there at the foot of the bed. Luna packs her suitcase, and Sam squeezes my foot once he sees I'm awake.

"Morning," he says, and I grunt in response.

With my head resting on my hands, I watch Luna as the sun trickles in through her blinds. A sweat builds on her neck and forehead while she's organizing outfits and makeup until the rest of her stuff arrives in Mexico. This is my last day with her.

I sit up in bed with the pillows behind me. Nellie jumps on the bed and sits in my lap. She leans into the pets, really wanting her chin scratched. I oblige. Then I remember that this is my last day with Nellie, too. So many goodbyes in one day.

"Do you want a cat?" I ask and both Sam and Luna look up from what they're doing.

"What?" Luna asks.

"Sam, do you want a cat?" I ask. "I can help you take care of her if you want."

"I don't know the first thing about taking care of a cat, Nai."

"It's easy. All you do is feed her and clean her litter box and love her. Is Ms. Tish allergic?"

"Not that I know of."

"So there's no reason you can't have a cat."

"Nai, I—"

"It's just that they may put her down if no one takes her, and she's a perfect kitty who doesn't deserve that." I lift Nellie into the air and let her feet dangle before cradling her. Why would someone hurt something as precious as her?

"Can I think about it first?"

"You can have her stuff. Her bed, some food, her toys," Luna offers.

"Y'all are ganging up on me."

"I mean we don't want her to be homeless when she could have a home. Mom hates me and doesn't want animals in the house."

"Let me think about it first."

"Can you think fast?" I grimace. Luna leaves tomorrow, and Nellie needs a home today.

"Keep her for a month," Luna suggests. "If you hate her, then give her to the shelter."

"Y'all are not gonna take no for an answer?"

"Sorry, Sammy. You're our only hope."

He leans his head back and groans. "Fine. I'll take her."

"Yay!" I clap my hands, but Nellie shifts so I have to stop. I crawl on the bed to lay my head on Sam's shoulder. "Thank you Sammy. You're the best."

"I know I am. And you better help me."

"I will come over whenever you need me. I promise."

Looking down at the angel I'm cradling, I may not be able to keep Luna, but I can keep a living reminder of her.

Mrs. Hernandez orders breakfast for everyone from a cafe on the square. While we eat, Luna hunts for Nellie's carrier to transport her to the house. Because Nellie is perfect, treats will her into the carrier so we don't have to fight to put her in there. Once all of Nellie's supplies have been gathered, we stand in Luna's room looking at each other. This is it. Our last goodbye. Tears have already started to sting my face.

"Naima, already," Luna groans. I wrap my arms around her shoulders and squeeze her tight. I never want to let her go, and I mean that in every way possible.

Sam wraps himself around Luna and me, and we hold onto each other for a very long time, but not long enough. It can never be enough. When Sam pulls away, Luna is crying. I wipe her tears.

"Look what y'all did to me," she says.

We did nothing but love her.

Mr. and Mrs. Hernandez gives us equally tight hugs.

"Remember to visit," Mr. Hernandez tells me while I'm hugging him. I start crying when I think about how he's always been a fun tío to me.

"I will," I say. I don't know how I'll go to Mexico, but if Luna's there, I'll find a way.

Luna walks us out, and we place Nellie in her carrier in the backseat. Sam starts the Jeep, and I go to hug Luna one last time before I ~~never see her again~~ see her again one day in the near future.

"I love you, Naima," she says, though it's muffled from the hug.

"I love you, Luna." I break away and take one last look at her. Her face is pink and slightly swollen from all the tears. I kiss her cheek then sniffle. "Let me know when you make it safely."

"I will. Hasta luego."

"Ojalá, pronto."

"Ojalá."

After one last hug, I join Sam in the Jeep. We wave at Luna as we back out of her driveway. Nellie's screeching in the backseat so I grab her carrier and set it in my lap. I stick my finger in the grates, and she licks them before using them to scratch her chin and neck. She's scared just like the rest of us, looking for some comfort and familiarity.

When we get to Sam's house, as promised, I help him set up Nellie's food, water, and litter box. Ms. Tish is home and seems excited about the cat so that makes me hopeful that Nellie can stay. I play with her for a little bit before leaving them to go back to my room. Dragging myself to my house and up the stairs, I climb into bed and weep.

This is growing up, I remind myself. This is what it means to be an adult.

Chapter Twenty-Three
Naima

She wore a bright floral dress with two French braids with ribbons on the end. Was the dress pink or yellow? It doesn't matter. She stood out. Mainly because we were told dresses were to be worn at church, but she wore one to school. She didn't understand the social rules, and neither did I. Since we sat in alphabetical order, her desk was near mine. While everyone else sneered and mocked and chanted Trump slogans, I waved at her. She waved back.

⎯⎯ℓℓℓ⎯⎯

She waved goodbye to me and Sam in the Jeep, tears streaming down her face. Hair no longer in braids but down in loose waves.

⎯⎯ℓℓℓ⎯⎯

Tears fell down her face when she darkened my door. She slid into the bed beside me and held me as I cried into her shoulder. There were no words to fill the sudden absence of Dad's death.

~ele~

For the first few months she was here, we didn't speak. We didn't need to. I waved at her. She waved back. I left a seat for her beside me at the cafeteria table. She took it. She waved me over at recess to show me videos on the phone she snuck into school. We hid by the bushes and laughed at the videos where the comedy translated across languages.

~ele~

We laugh as she's experimenting with makeup. First on herself then on me. We laugh as we dance at Homecoming, Winter Formal, Junior Prom, Senior Prom. We laugh and dance and hold each other.

~ele~

She smiles on the phone and holds up the tiny black kitty she got from the shelter today. She cradles it in her arm and rocks it back and forth. I tell her about my therapy appointment. About how it's helping to talk to someone about the pain of loss.

I hugged her when her first boyfriend broke up with her and her second and her third. Confused by how they couldn't see how amazing she was and why they didn't want to spend everyday of their life with her when that's all I wanted.

She smiles in Patricia's face looking happy, confident, and free. They're bumping shoulders as they leave Wonderlust. She returns with an even brighter smile on her face.

"He likes you, Naima," she practically yells into the screen, and I want to burst from the possibility of more love entering my life.

"You're my best friend Naima," she says as the eleven year old with French braids, the thirteen year old experimenting with heatless curls, the sixteen year old with the messy bun, the eighteen year old with wavy hair. "I love you."

Chapter Twenty-Four

Kamron

"You got the job," Laurel says, her voice bright and cheery. She goes on to say how impressed she was with my interview and how excited she is that we'll be working together soon. I'm in my car outside of Naima's house. She didn't answer my text this morning, but the last time I saw her she said to come over today.

"Can I take some time to think about it?" I ask. It's only after the words are out that I realize I should've said it smoother.

"Oh, okay," she says, taken aback. "How about til after the holiday? Is that enough time?"

"That's perfect. Thanks for calling. This is a really exciting opportunity," I say, saving myself from earlier.

When we hang up, I'm left with an impending sense of dread. This is what I wanted right? To get a job so I wouldn't have to leave Mississippi and Naima? Why am I not happier about it?

I shake my head when I get out of the car. I'm tripping. Obviously, this *is* an exciting opportunity because I can stay with Naima for as long as I want.

When I walk up to Naima's bedroom door, it's closed so I knock on it. Normally, I walk right in, but since she hasn't responded to me, I don't want to overwhelm her. Hesitantly, I open the door, and the room is dark. She usually wakes up and opens her blackout curtains but not today.

"Naima?" I ask, ambling towards the bed. I sit at the foot and notice the lump curled up around the pillows. Placing my hand on it, she shifts, stretching her legs out from the fetal position.

"Hey," I say gently, trying to reach her.

"She should be in New Orleans now," she mumbles, looking at her clock on the nightstand. It's a few minutes after noon.

Unsure about what to do next, I climb into her bed and snuggle up behind her. She lays her arm over mine and presses it tighter into her body.

"She's gone," she says before a low wail leaves her body and then she curls in around my arm, sobbing into herself.

I tighten my grip around her to comfort her, but it's no use. She kicks, screams, and cries, and I have to let her. No matter how devastating it sounds. I still hold onto her so she knows that I'm here...while I still can be.

Once the tears stop, the soft snores tell me that she's done for now. I kiss her temple before going downstairs to grab some water and snacks for her and wait until she wakes up. Her phone lights up so I check it. It's Sam asking if she's okay to come over for the cat. When did he get a cat? I answer him, telling him it's me, she's asleep, and I'll tell her to text him when she wakes up. I haven't forgotten about Sam being in love with my girlfriend, but right now, he's not my top priority. She is.

She stirs beside me before struggling to open her eyes. They're swollen from crying. Instead she reaches her arms over my body and lays her head on my belly.

"I got you some water," I say, rubbing her back. I hand the cup to her, and she gulps the entire thing.

"Thank you," she rasps.

I slide down onto the bed until we're face to face. I wipe her puffy cheeks and stare into her reddened eyes. I know it makes her uncomfortable, but it's temporary. "Is there anything you need from me?"

"Can you hold me?" she asks, her chin wobbling.

I wrap my arms around her, pulling her to my chest. I kiss the satin scarf that loosely covers her head and don't let go of her even as my arm falls asleep. She goes in and out of sleep until she's ready to talk to me. When she does, it's almost night. Luna and her family should've made it to Mexico by now.

"Thank you,' she tells me again.

She reaches up to caress my face, and I kiss her fingers.

"Are you hungry? Can I get you something to eat?" I offer.

She shakes her head no then she stares into space, tears filling her eyes.

"Hey, hey, what is it? What's wrong?"

She looks up at me with her wobbling chin.

"You can tell me," I reassure her.

"I keep seeing her over and over again. It's like my brain's replaying everything like a movie. I remember more about my fifth grade classroom that I thought I did. How much I relied on Luna during quarantine. Our first sleepover. Everything is there, and I keep going back to it, and it takes me to a new memory I forgot. She's everywhere inside of me," she says.

I try to make sense of the fragments she's speaking in.

"You think I'm crazy," she says.

"No, no, I promise. I'm listening."

"Like when I close my eyes, I'm back there." She closes her eyes trying to explain what she means. "I'm sitting at my fifth grade desk, looking at Luna on the first day she came. I can taste" —she smacks her lips—"plátanos and that reminds me of the first time I was at one of her family barbecues and had plátanos for the first time and ate an entire plate of them."

"It sounds like time traveling or astral projection," I say.

"It's how I experience memory."

"Like how stars are memory?"

The first time I sat and talked with Naima on her porch, she told me about everything she loved: Little Mix, her dad, and stars. She was so excited talking about the stars. It felt like the first time I saw the real her, uninhibited. Her smile. Her tears. Her everything. I knew then I wouldn't be happy unless I knew her every thought, dream, feeling.

"Yeah, it's like stars are here and not here at the same time," she answers.

"And Luna is always here" —I caress my thumb against her temple— "and here" —I place my hand over her heart—"even when she's not here."

Naima manages the tiniest smile. "I guess you're right."

I rub her shoulder. I hope I'm right, too.

We flip through streaming apps trying to find something to soothe Naima. I pick a comedy special figuring that the only way to balance out crying is laughter. It works...some. When she settles into bed and sleeps again, I slip downstairs to head home. Ms. Shunda is standing in the kitchen.

"Hey baby, how is she?" she asks.

"She's asleep."

Her eyebrows knit together. Her mouth thins into a frown. She takes a sip of the wine she's holding. "Is she talking?"

"Some."

She nods and takes another sip. "When her dad died, she didn't say anything for weeks. Just hours of crying and sleeping. She wouldn't eat." She shakes her head and wipes the corner of her eye. Then she smiles. "I'm glad you're here."

"Me, too," I say, knowing that I'm on the fence about accepting Laurel's job offer. I'm already past Pop's deadline. It's either take this job or go home.

She places her hand over mine. "Okay honey. Drive safe."

"I will. Have a good night." I smile.

Once I'm in my car, I lean my head against the steering wheel. What is Naima going to do if I leave? Who's going to lay with her all day in bed? Luna's gone. She'll be in college. Why did I fight all summer to stay when I could've told her the truth? If she knew, right now she could've been prepared for us both to leave. Now? Will it ever be the right time for her?

I crank up the car and ease down the gravel driveway headed back to town wondering if Naima will ever forgive me.

Chapter Twenty-Five

Kamron

"Have you decided what you gone do?" Nana asks, hobbling over to the couch to sit beside me. I've told her, Amaya, and Jada that I got the job. I haven't told my parents yet because I still don't know if I'll take it.

"No ma'am," I admit.

Nana sits down beside me and places her hand on my thigh. Her pale fingers squeeze my knee. "How long that lady give you to decide?"

"Til after the holiday," I say. Today's July fourth so I have until Monday.

"What you thinking?" she asks. Her blue eyes pierce mine.

I'm thinking I never want to leave Naima. I'm thinking there's no way I can afford to stay. I lean back against the sofa and exhale.

"I don't know."

She nods then asks, "Okay, why can't you stay?"

"If I take this job, I can see Naima whenever I'm off, but I won't have time to dedicate to my art."

She hums a deep affirmation. "And if you leave?"

"I can devote time to my art. I get to see my parents, but I won't have time for Naima."

"So either way, it's gonna cost you something: art or Naima?" she asks.

She gets it! I sit up and nod towards her.

"Did I ever tell you about me and your grandpa?" she asks.

"Yes ma'am."

Nana and Grandpa grew up together in San Francisco but didn't date again until after their first marriages. Both had already had kids. Nana had Amaya, and Grandpa had Aunt Maxine and Uncle Junior.

"We dated after high school. It was real quick. Just a summer. He knew I was going to college, and he didn't want to stop me. We spent nearly every day of that summer together, squeezing every ounce of love we could out of each other until I had to leave. And then I met Zachariah in college, and Reginald married Lily and I thought that was it, but as you can see—."

She waves her hand around, but I'm not over the fact that Naima could find someone else in college and forget all about me. She could *marry* someone else. My brain fills with all the times Sam's looked at her with so much love in his eyes. If I leave, he can make his move. He can be with her. He—

"Kamron." Nana places her hand over mine. "If y'all are meant to be, you'll find your way back to each other. Don't worry about the how. Just trust that God will make it happen."

"Yes, ma'am," I say to her even though I'm not sure I believe it. How do I know if I break up with Naima that she'll ever want to speak to me again? That she'll ever love me again? I have to stay, but is it right to only stay so Naima can't end up with someone else? Is it right to give up my dream of being an artist to help Naima with her dream of being a biochemist?

I only have a couple of days to decide what to do.

"You'll figure it out," Nana reassures me, patting my knee, before trying to get up. I help her up, and she limps toward Amaya to help her with the food for today's cookout.

Whatever I'm going to do, I only have a few days left to decide.

Chapter Twenty-Six

Naima

Luna's been gone for two days now, and I've cried a normal amount of times when you lose your best friend in the whole entire world. Kamron invited me to his July fourth cookout thinking that being around other people would cheer me up. Everybody thinks the best thing for me to do right now is to move on from Luna. Maybe not move on, but to focus on other things besides her not being here, but what's so wrong about lingering in the pain of her absence? It fucking hurts to wake up and know that I can't hug Luna again. Why can't I be sad about that for at least two whole days?

I brought Markese along to get him out of the house. Unlike me, he loves socializing and being the center of attention so I hope that people will pay attention to him and forget about me. Kamron waits for us at the front door. I trudge over, and he wraps his arm around me. His neck smells like sweat and the sandalwood soap he uses. Although it's sticky, I lay my head against his neck and slump into him. He rubs my back and then places his hands on my jaw and neck, facing my head towards his. "Are you feeling better?"

What a stupid question. How can I feel any better when Luna is gone?

I don't say anything. I can't say anything. What is there to say? I shrug. That's the only accurate reply. A shrug.

He wraps his arm around me and whispers in my ear. "Thank you for coming over."

I shrug again. Amaya's in the kitchen, and she waves at me. I wave back and attempt to smile, but my face is too heavy, too droopy, too sad. I sit at the bar window between the living room and kitchen and lay my head on the smooth cold granite.

Amaya walks over with a refrigerated bottle of water. "Hey Niece," she says softly and slides the bottle to me. I lift my eyes but not my head to her. "It's good seeing you."

I nod. She rubs my elbow then walks back to the kitchen to cook. Behind me, Markese laughs at some older men telling him the rules to dominoes. I grab the water, slink down the hall to Kamron's room, and slide into his bed. His pillows smell like the sweet curl cream he uses. I told him to switch to foam. It'd make his pillows less greasy, but he didn't listen. I turn the pillow over to the less greasy side and lay there until tears start to soak the cotton. Folding my knees into my chest, I cry.

When I wake up, I grab the bottle of water and drink it until the plastic folds in on itself. I grab my phone out of my pocket and see the messages. Kamron asked where I was and Sam asked what I was doing. I told Kamron I'm in his room, and Sam that I'm at a bbq. As the dots appear on Sam's message, Kamron knocks on his door and lets himself in. He lays on the bed facing me and interlaces his fingers with mine. With his touch, it's like my heart tries to spark, but the fire doesn't catch. It's way too cold and damp.

Instead of speaking, he wraps his arm around me and pulls me into his chest. I lay there until my face overheats, and I have to pull away for air. His thumb caresses my cheek, and I look up at him.

"You can stay here as long as you like."

I nod. He squeezes me again before letting go and returning to the party. I roll over on my back and pick up my phone to see a series of Sam's messages.

SAM: Is it important

Can you come over

I think the cat ran away

I looked everywhere but I can't find her

Please Nai I need your help

As much as I want to help, I doubt I can drag my body out the door.

I'm at Kamron's. It'll be a while.

I start thinking of tiny Nellie alone and out in the woods filled with coyotes, dogs, and foxes. She won't make it. She's just a baby.

Fine. I'm coming.

I sit up, close my eyes, and breathe. Save Nellie. That seems like an attainable goal for today.

I text Kamron that I'm leaving and ask him to bring Markese home. When I open the door, Kamron's already there.

"Are you alright? Do you need me to do anything?"

I place my hand on his eager chest. "Nellie ran away. I'm gonna help Sam find her."

"Oh." He steps back. "Sam."

"Yeah. And Nellie."

"Do you want me to come?"

"No," I say. "Stay. I'll see you later."

Before I leave the hallway, he grabs me and plants a kiss on my lips. It discombobulates me, and I shake my head before saying, "Bye."

Sam's standing outside his house looking in the bushes for Nellie. He stops and walks towards me when he sees me pull up in Mom's Equinox.

"I've been looking for her all morning," he says as soon as I open the door.

I walk past him into the house and straight to his bed to lay down.

"What are you doing? She's outside somewhere."

"When was the last time you saw her?" I ask.

"Last night. When she ate."

"Has anyone opened a door or window since then?"

"I mean I was just outside looking for her."

"She's probably not outside," I tell him.

When Luna first got Nellie, she stowed away behind her dresser's drawers for a week acclimating to the new environment. Over the years, especially when she's scared, she's found the tiniest crevices to stick herself in.

I roll over and look at his chest of drawers. "Check your drawers."

His eyebrows knit together.

"She's probably hiding somewhere in the house."

He checks the drawers, but she's not there. He knocks on Ms. Tish's door. She's off for the holiday. He checks her dresser, closet, and under her bed. Then we check the cabinets, behind the fridge, and in the dishwasher. (It's surprising where cats can squeeze themselves into.) We check the sofa cushions and the cubbies in the entertainment center. When I lift up the flap behind the recliner, I hear the tiniest meow.

"Nellie?"

She meows again before I see her black tail sticking out the side of the recliner. I don't know how she got up there, but when she hears my voice, she starts to come down.

"Gatita." I scoop her up and cradle her. She curls into my arms.

"You found her?" Sam says.

"Yeah. Can you grab her treats?"

Upon hearing the T word, Nellie reorients and hops out of my arm. She stands on the floor and screams.

"Alright. I hear you," Sam says, grabbing the container of treats from the kitchen counter. He scatters some on the floor, and Nellie rushes over.

I plop onto the couch now that the crisis has been averted. While Nellie nibbles on the treats, Sam joins me.

"Thanks for helping me find Nell," he says.

"Nell?"

"Yeah. Nellie reminded me of a horse."

"So you shorten all N words, huh?" I smirk.

"Nai," he groans.

The smile leaves my face. Teasing Sam isn't even half the fun it used to be without Luna here.

"It's nice to see you again. You've been—"

"—yeah," I cut him off.

"How was the bbq?"

"Loud. Kamron's trying. I'm grateful, but he—"

"—he's not Luna," Sam finishes.

"He's not Luna." I smoosh my lips. Nobody can replace Luna.

"I miss her too." The corner of his mouth curves into a

sympathetic smile.

"Have you cried?" I ask.

"You don't have to cry to feel sad."

"But you have to let the sadness out. Otherwise it stays here." I lay my hand over his heart. "That's not good for you."

He lifts my hand from his chest and places it on my thigh. Then he lays his hand on top of mine. "You don't have to worry about me."

I scoff. "I worry about everybody, everywhere, all the time."

He chuckles softly then studies my face. "Do you want to stay over? Hang out?"

"I can stay for a little bit," I say.

I don't remember the last time we've spent alone together. I'm usually with Luna or Kamron. He's with Dixie, Marcus, or Darius.

He smiles. "Cooking show or cartoons?"

"Cooking."

"Okay. Have you eaten?"

I think back, but all I can remember is that bottle of water I guzzled. "No?"

"You want me to make you your popcorn."

"Please," I say. He knows how I like it.

Chapter Twenty-Seven

Naima

When I walk over to check on ~~Nellie~~ Nell, Sam's on the floor with pieces of a scratching post all around him. As I open the screen door, he looks up at me, "There you are. I need your help."

"What are you doing?"

"We're building this." He flips the instructions upside down, continues to gaze at it, before handing it to me.

"We?" I look at the paper that illustrates how to put the pieces together to form a cactus scratching post.

"Yeah. All these pieces look alike."

I sit beside him on the ground and look from the sheet to the pieces. One, they don't all look alike; they're different sizes, and two, the pieces have letters on the bottom of them that correspond to a letter on the paper. When I show him that, I start handing him the pieces and letting him assemble the post. After about twenty minutes, Nell has a two feet cactus scratching post with pink flowers on top.

Sam goes to find her, picks her up, and drops her by the post. She sniffs it briefly before walking away.

"Maybe catnip?" I suggest. "Where's the bag Luna left?"

Sam hands it to me, and I sprinkle it on the scratching post. Now Nell cares and sniffs on the scratching post, licking the bits of catnip she can find and eventually digging her nails into the post, scratching and stretching her body. I clap, and Sam high fives me.

"Has she been hiding a lot?" I ask him. It's been a couple of days since he panicked about her missing.

"Some. Usually we can find her pretty quickly."

"So I'm guessing the scratching post means she's staying?" I lean against the kitchen island.

"Mom likes having her. Nell sleeps at the foot of her bed."

"And you? Do you like having her?"

He shrugs. "She's pretty cool, I guess."

"You guess? She's perfect. How can you say that?"

"I wouldn't call cleaning a litter box perfect."

"It's the price you have to pay for perfection."

Nell saunters past us and stretches in the light of the front door before curling into a ball to take a nap.

"She does that a lot." Sam juts his thumb out at her. "She finds a window or door and naps there for hours."

"She needs her sun," I explain to him. Who doesn't like a warm cozy nap? "Have you been speaking to her in Spanish?"

Sam groans.

"She comes from a bilingual household. She needs both languages," I remind him.

"It seems like the only word she cares about is 'treats.'"

I flinch expecting Nell to start shrieking, but she doesn't. Maybe she didn't hear him.

"Spanish will help her feel safe and welcomed. Like 'Hola, Gatita. ¿Cómo estás?' and then she meows in response. And then you talk to her and call her beautiful and amazing and smart."

"She don't need all that."

"Yes she does. It'll boost her self-esteem."

"She's a cat!"

"And?"

A smile tugs the corner of his lips, and he shakes his head. "She's fine. I promise you that."

"I don't know. You take her from her home, change her name, and force her to stop speaking her native language." I look him up and down. "Sounds about right."

"Naima," he groans, and I can't help but burst out into a giggle. "You're the worst. You know that?"

"If by worst, you mean best then yes I am." I lift my chin proudly.

He shakes his head then smiles. After a few seconds his smile fades, "Have you um...have you talked to Luna?"

"No," I sigh. "I'm waiting for her to adjust."

It's been almost a week since she's been gone. I'm waiting for me to adjust, too. So far, it hasn't been going well.

Sam's brow furrows, "You haven't texted her or called?"

"Should I?" I ask.

"It wouldn't hurt."

We sit on the couch, and I video call her through WhatsApp. Thankfully, Oaxaca is in the same time zone so I don't have to figure out what time it is there. It's a little after two. After a few rings, she picks up. She's a few shades tanner than when she left, and her wavy hair is in a ponytail. There's music and laughter in the background.

"Luna!" I wave.

"Hey girl," she says. The smile brightening her face relieves me. "I can't talk for long. What's up?"

"We just wanted to see how you're doing," I say, and Sam waves at the screen.

"Hey Sam. I'm fine. We're staying at my tío's and he threw a party," she gestures behind her. "How have y'all been?"

"I've been great." I fake a smile to not worry her, but Sam glances at me and frowns.

"We miss you," he says.

Luna pouts then says, "I miss you, too." Her attention is divided between us and a person off-camera speaking Spanish to her. I can only get bits and pieces of it, not enough to make a coherent sentence.

"I gotta go y'all," Luna says. "Thanks for calling."

Before I can tell her I love her and goodbye, her face is gone from the screen. Sam rubs my shoulder because the devastation of it all is probably already apparent on my face.

"I gotta go," I tell him. He doesn't even try to stop me. I'm sure he already knows.

I shuffle to my house as tears drizzle down my cheeks. Thankfully, I make it to the room before the downpour.

Chapter Twenty-Eight

Kamron

Mama's been blowing up my phone nonstop. It doesn't help that it's the day that I have to give Laurel my decision. I've been going over and over in my head what I want to do. After the fifth call, Mama leaves a voicemail.

"Kamron, sweetheart," she says in a stern voice. "I know you're not ignoring your mother. Call me back. You'll want to hear this."

I lean my head against the couch. I'm days past their deadline to let them know if I'm staying in Mississippi or not. What could Mama possibly have to say to change my mind?

Despite wanting to hide from them until I figure out what I want to do, I call Mama.

"So you *were* ignoring my call," she says when she answers.

"Mama," I groan. "There's a lot going on."

"Like what?"

I clench my teeth, wondering if I should tell her like this.

Maybe it'll stop the back to back calling. "I got a job."

"Oh," she seems taken aback. "Well I guess you don't want to hear my news then."

"What is it, Mama?"

"Peri said yes!" she announces giddily.

"What?" I ask. What is she talking about?

"Peri. Periwinkle Moonchild said yes to taking you on as an apprentice. Now you won't be paid, but you'll be home so you won't have anything to worry about."

"Wait, what are you saying Mama?" I ask. This can't be true. I could work with Periwinkle Moonchild.

"I'm saying if you come home, you'll work with Peri and who knows? Maybe you can exhibit with her. Maybe you can have your own show."

"Are you serious?" I can't believe this is happening right now.

"I'm very serious. All you have to do is come home," she says.

"Okay," I acquiesce.

"Okay?" she asks, confirming what I'm trying to say.

This is everything I've been working towards the past few years. This is *my* dream. Unlike the job offer where there was so much hesitation, doubt, and denial, there is immediate certainty. I have to do this.

"I'm going home," I confirm.

I'm going to say goodbye to Naima. I'm going to break her heart. After almost two years together, I only have forty-two days left with her.

"Do you want me to send a moving van today or maybe on Monday?" Mama asks eagerly.

"I'll drive home, Mama. Can you just give me until the end of August?"

"Kamron, I—"

"I promise," I cut her off. "I'll go home and stay home this time."

"Okay," she sighs. "No more extensions. I'll tell Peri that you want to start in September."

"Thank you, Mama," I say and I mean it.

When we hang up, I immediately email Laurel to thank her for the job but ultimately decline it. It's like a load's been lifted off of my chest. It wasn't until I got another offer that I realized how much I don't want to work a full-time job or live in Jackson even if it means I get to stay with Naima. Unfortunately, here's the bad part. I also have to tell Naima.

I haven't seen her since she rushed out of my house a few days ago to help Sam and his cat. I've tried texting and video calling, but she rarely answers. I understand she's sad about Luna leaving, but I want to be there for her, too, and it feels like she's pushing me away. I text her again to let her know I'm coming over, and before she gives me a response, I get into the car and drive to her house.

When I get to her room, the door is closed so I knock tentatively before entering. When I open it, it's dark but a rank smell hangs in the air. Naima stares at her phone as it lights up her face.

"Naima?"

She turns towards me. Half of her hair is out of the braids.

"What are you doing here?" she asks flatly.

I'm not saying I expected a warm welcome, but I hoped it would be warmer than this.

"Just wanted to check up on you." I sit on the edge of the bed and reach for her leg. She tucks it under herself. The smell is stronger now like she hasn't showered in a couple of days.

"I'm fine," she grumbles, turning her attention back to her phone.

"When was the last time you left your room?" I ask.

She scowls at me.

"I think it's a good idea to—" I say before she interrupts.

"Why do you get to decide what's good for me?" She tumbles out of the bed and runs to the bathroom, shutting the door.

It wasn't what I was expecting, but I push away my shock and knock on the door gently. "Naima?"

"Stop trying to fix me!" she yells.

"I'm not," I whisper. I just want to spend what little time we have left together.

"I don't want you here. Leave!"

She doesn't want me here. My breath shakes, but I clear my throat.

"Okay Naima. If that's what you want."

I stand there watching the door, waiting, hoping for...I don't know what. For her to say sorry? For her to not be sad anymore? For her to realize that I'm leaving, and we're wasting the little time we have left? She doesn't open the door so I leave and give her exactly what she wants.

Chapter Twenty-Nine

Naima

CHAPTER THIRTY

Kamron

Hey, this is Sam. I got your number from the group chat. Naima told me what happened. Im sorry man. She gets like this when bad shit happens. She was MEAN after her dad died. Dont take it personal.

Chapter Thirty-One

Naima

It took at least a day to finish taking down my hair, shower, clean my piercing, and ask to see Kamron. He said yes. I stand outside his door watching the moths fly around his porch light before I knock. He answers it within seconds.

"Hey." I fidget with my fingers.

"You can come in." He leans against the door to let me pass. He's in a t-shirt, boxers, and his glasses.

I'm not tryna stay long so I start, "I'm sorry."

I exhale, looking up at the ceiling thinking about all the things I want to say. I practiced saying so many things, but none of them felt right.

"You didn't deserve to be yelled at. I do want to see you. I do want you around. I um," I sniffle as tears start to fill my eyes. "I wasn't ready. I didn't want you to see me like that."

His thumb wipes away the tear on my cheek, and I close my eyes thinking about how I don't deserve his kindness after I was so cruel to him. Why is he always so kind and accepting towards me? Why does he keep loving me?

"Thank you for apologizing," he says softly.

I nod then sniffle, my head still downturned. "If you need some time, I get it. I'll leave."

"Hey." He grabs my wrist as I'm about to walk past him. He wraps his arm around me and pulls me into a hug. His arm tightens around me, and I feel more and more unworthy of his comfort. I weep in his arms.

"Naima." He breaks the hug and holds my face.

"I know you hate me. I'm sorry I get like this. I wish I could control it."

I can only imagine the blistering bumbling mess that I look like right now. His eyes soften towards me, and I struggle to breath through the avalanche of tears.

"I could never hate you." My head sinks, and he lowers his gaze to try and maintain eye contact. "I went to see you because I missed you. I don't care what you look like or what you're going through, I wanna be there."

His hand grabs mine, and our fingers interlace.

"I love *you*, Naima. All of you."

I nod.

"And I...I don't want to tell you what's good for you, but I wanna see you. I know you need your space, but can I come over once a week? We can still do stuff as a group. With Markese and Eric...and Sam. We still have a few more weeks of summer."

"Okay," I nod, then tap my finger to his chest. "*You* plan our weekly things, and I'll be there."

"I can do that," he chuckles. "Can you stay?"

He's in boxers, clearly not expecting company. Plus, the TV is paused on some show that he's a good bit into. "You look busy. I don't want to—"

"Naima, I want you here with me. Please."

When he says it like that, there's really no arguing so I nod.

"We don't have to watch anything. We can just lay down in my bed if you want."

"Okay," I say.

I slip off my shoes and follow him to his room. We crawl into bed and cuddle on top of the comforter. Two perfect spoons. His arm tightens around my belly, and I hold onto it for support, pushing it further into my body as we breathe in and out. His breath tickles my neck before he kisses the spot behind my ear softly, slowly. When he kisses another spot on my neck, my eyes shut, and I bite my lip. His fingers travel up my belly and under my bralette. My breath catches. I grab his thigh pulling his body closer to mine. We grind against each other before I turn around and kiss him. My tongue urges its way into his mouth, and once inside a moan escapes. Kamron breaks away and kisses my forehead. Caressing my cheek, he stares at me like I'm the most precious thing he's ever held, and for a second, I believe him.

Chapter Thirty-Two

Kamron

Jada brainstormed ideas with me for things that could help lift Naima's mood. So I brought Phase 10, Dominoes, and Monopoly. The Monopoly's a stretch, but I figured I'd try. When I get to Naima's, only my and Ms. Shunda's cars are in the driveway. I glance towards Sam's house, and his Jeep isn't there. Hopefully that means he's sitting this one out.

I don't know how to feel about him being in love with my girlfriend. I can't say I blame him, but I'm uneasy knowing that they spend so much time alone together. He lives next door! At any moment, he could make a move on her, and what would she do? Reciprocate? End their friendship? Then that's three of us that she's losing, and I don't know if she can handle that, but if Sam wanted to act on his feelings, wouldn't he have already? He has a girlfriend, and he doesn't seem like the kind to sabotage multiple relationships at once.

I shake my head and walk towards the porch with the boxes in tow. Maybe Sam won't make a move on Naima, but I can watch him, just in case. Naima sees me walking past the kitchen window and opens the door for me since my arms are full.

"Thank you," I say, and she smiles. I want to check-in with her and ask if she's okay, but I still remember her yelling at me a few days ago. She remembers it too. Her head is dipped low because she's also unsure about how to move forward after that.

"Is it okay if I hug you?" I ask, and she nods. Tentatively, I wrap my arm around her and breathe in her sweet honey skin. Her back rises and falls in my arms. When I break the hug, I caress her cheek and hope that she understands that I'm here with her and for her, even if she doesn't always want me to be.

She looks up towards me briefly before turning her attention to the table. "What'd you bring?" she asks, sitting the boxes beside each other. "Phase 10?"

"You've never played?" I ask. She shakes her head. "It's real easy. I'll show you."

Mentally, I pump my fist because I'm excited I get to show her another thing that she'll remember me by. Baseball, bowling, and now Phase 10. What if this becomes her new favorite thing?

Markese walks downstairs and daps me up.

"We playing dominoes?" he asks, then turns to Naima. "I'm gone whoop you."

"You wish!" Naima shoves him.

He squares up to her and towers over her. "I'm bigger than you now, Lil Dip."

"Mom!" she yells, and Markese cowers.

When Ms. Shunda comes out of her room, she hugs me and asks, "How you doing baby?" To Naima and Markese she says, "Y'all too old for this."

"She started it."

"I did not!"

Ms. Shunda rolls her eyes, and I smile thinking about how close-knit and playful her family is. She walks to the fridge and grabs a pitcher of sweet tea, pouring herself a drink. "What we playing?"

"I brought Phase 10, Dominoes, and Monopoly."

Her face scrunches up on Monopoly. Yep. Should've left that one at home. She walks over to the table and flips over the Phase 10 card tin.

"I haven't played this since I was a little girl," she says, sipping the tea.

"A Black man created the game," I tell her.

"I know. That's why my parents bought it."

"We can start with that if you want," Naima offers, walking closer to the table.

"Does Eric want to play?" Ms. Shunda asks.

"Eric!" Naima yells.

After a few seconds, he pops his head out of the downstairs

guest room. "What?"

"We're having a game night. Come on."

"Ugh," he groans, shutting the door and eventually emerging in a silk pajama lounge set and matching durag.

We gather around the table. I'm in front of the window; Naima is to my right. Ms. Shunda and Markese are to my left, and Eric sits across from me. I shuffle the cards and deal ten out to everybody, placing the rest of the deck in the center and flipping over a card.

"So how do we play?" Naima asks, looking at the cards in her hands.

Before I can begin, Ms. Shunda speaks, "If I remember correctly, there's an instruction card and you have to complete all ten phases. Right?" She turns to me.

"Yeah," I say, searching the tin for the instruction card, and passing one to each side of the table. I read the instructions that each person must complete each phase before proceeding to the next one and then further explain, "If Naima gets Phase 1 and the rest of us don't by the time the turn ends, she goes to Phase 2, and we all stay at Phase 1 until we complete it."

Everyone around the table nods.

"How do we know that a phase has ended?" Naima asks.

"When someone runs out of cards. So everybody has to do Phase 1 which is 2 sets of 3 cards so like three sevens and three fours completes the phase. Each turn we're going to draw a card and discard one. Usually, my family plays that part like

Uno where we try to match the color or number with the card on top of the discard pile, but people play that part differently. Once you've completed your phase and gotten rid of your cards, it ends the round for everyone."

"We need to keep score. Markese, grab some paper and a pen out that drawer." Ms. Shunda commands, and Markese obeys.

Naima nods, still staring at her cards. "I think I'm getting it. I'll figure it out as we're playing."

"Yeah me, too," Eric says.

"I'm confused," Markese adds.

Ms. Shunda rubs his arm. "I got you, baby."

There are a few more questions as we play the round, and I try my best to answer them all. Ms. Shunda fills in on things that I forget. I'm not saying I'm a prophet or anything, but Naima finishes Phase 1 and gets out before the rest of us have a chance to finish. I had three twos , two sixes, and two elevens. I just needed one more of either to complete my round.

The pair of elevens puts me in last place, but that doesn't matter. Naima's leg bounces on the chair, and her brow furrows while looking at her cards. She's so into this game, I can't help but to smile. Every time someone lays a card in the discard pile, she bites down on her lip, probably strategizing her next move to beat us. I don't even care if I lose at this point. As long as I can distract Naima and make her happy again for just one night, that's a win.

We catch up to Naima at the dreaded Phase 7. She's been

stuck here for three rounds. I don't know what it is about Phase 7, but it caused fights when I was younger. It feels impossible to beat. You have to get two sets of four, and you can only have a max of ten cards in your hand. Maybe it's because mathematically, two people can't go for the same number, and if you have, you won't complete your set. I don't know, but I move the cards around in my hand. I have a pair of fours, sevens, and nines.

Naima sighs *loudly*.

"Uh-oh, she's getting mad," Ms. Shunda teases.

"I'm not getting mad. I'm just frustrated." Naima slides her hand up to her temple and stares at the discard pile and her hand. I reach my hand across the table and touch her forearm. She looks up from the cards to me, offering a sad smile. At this point, I'll take whatever she gives me.

Markese is the one to break through Phase 7. It feels like we've been at this Phase for about as long as we've played the entire game. Before he ends the Phase, Ms. Shunda finishes too. She's been "teaching him how to play" by telling him what cards to get and using his hand to figure out what she should play. I'd call it cheating, but hey, this ain't my house.

Everyone completes their phase in the next round. Eric, Naima, and I on Phase 8, and Ms. Shunda and Markese on Phase 9.

"I'm gonna let you do these last two phases yourself, Markese," she says, patting his hand.

She's not slick. She wants to win.

It seems that we flip-flop this round with Eric, Naima, and I completing our phases. We're all on Phase 9 and then Naima and I go to Phase 10. I complete the phase first, but I still have cards so the round hasn't ended. Naima completes her phase and then playfully squints at me like we're battling it out. I grin back at her. Markese and Eric complete theirs before Markese runs out of cards. Because Naima, Markese, and I all completed Phase 10, we go by the scores. Naima beats me by 50 points and Markese by 20. Round one really messed me up.

I applaud her.

"Thank you," she says, bowing like she just finished a performance.

"We playing again?" Markese asks.

"No," everyone says in unison.

"But it was fun, right?" I ask.

"Yeah, it was fun." Naima smiles at me while getting up from her chair. She heads to the bathroom while everyone else reaches for their phone.

"Do y'all want pizza for dinner?" Ms. Shunda asks.

"Thin-crust!" Naima shouts from the bathroom.

Eric throws his hands in the air. "Who wants their pizza crunchy? Let me guess you think pineapple belongs on pizza, too!" he yells towards the bathroom.

The bathroom door flies open while the sink is running.

"It's sweet *and* savory," she says, emerging from the bathroom, shaking the water from her hands. Eric looks even more exasperated, rolling his eyes and exhaling. "Sorry some of us have *taste*."

"More like some of us *need* taste." He looks her up and down.

"Y'all keep arguing. I'm just gonna get a cheese and pepperoni. Do you want meat-lovers?" Ms. Shunda asks Naima who nods at her. Ms. Shunda finishes placing the order and then grabs her keys. "Let me know if y'all need anything else from town."

"Drive safe!" Naima blurts.

"I will," Ms. Shunda sad-smiles before leaving.

After a small break, we play dominoes. Everyone knows the basic concept of dominoes: match the number (and color) of the domino. Since I have the pieces, I ask, "Do y'all want to play Mexican Train?"

"We can," Eric says. "You gotta explain it."

So I explain the rules of the game to everyone.

"Why does the train have to be Mexican?" Naima asks, her face expressionless, and immediately my heart sinks. Does this remind her too much of Luna? Why didn't I think of that when I grabbed this? Why did I even suggest Mexican Train?

"I'm not sure," is all I can muster.

"Was it made in Mexico?" she asks.

I shrug so she pulls out her phone to find the truth herself. Eric and I shuffle the dominoes before we grab ten dominoes each.

"It was actually the US being racist," Naima says, while looking down at her phone. "Chinese laborers brought a similar game to Cuba and other places, and Cubans adapted it to dominoes and then the US were calling them Mexicans. Maybe some Mexicans played it, but you can never be sure."

"Thanks for the history lesson, Cuz," Eric says sarcastically.

"You're welcome." Naima scrunches her face in a forced smile.

Everyone's smiling, laughing, and joking. I'm glad that I was able to bring this to Naima and her family. We play dominoes until Ms. Shunda comes back with the pizza. While we're finishing the round, she takes a picture of us. With her phone over her heart, she says, "It's so nice seeing all y'all around my table having fun."

Naima, Eric, and Markese all roll their eyes.

"You two are going off to college, and it'll just be me and my baby boy." She squeezes Markese.

"Ma!" he groans.

College is only thirty-four days away for Naima. Thirty-four days to break her already broken heart. I glance over at her, biting on her lip while watching her family interact. She deserves to know, blindsiding her will only make it worse, but I'm not doing all this work to make her feel better just to tear her down again.

Once we finish the round, we sit in the living room and

around the kitchen counter eating pizza. When Naima bites into her pizza, there's an audible crunch.

"Cardboard-ass pizza," Eric mumbles.

"Shut up," Naima says with a full mouth.

"I bet you get it so you can have a whole pizza to herself."

She smiles and then Eric gasps, "You do!"

Naima laughs walking over to the couch. I'm about to follow her, but Eric stops me.

"Can I ask you a question?"

"Sure." I slide onto the bar stool beside him.

"What was it like living in California?"

I don't know why the question catches me off-guard, but something about it makes my chest loosen thinking about my life in California. Pops and I playing catch in our backyard. Mama treating me to Ettore's every Friday and Gunther's during the summer. Hearing Jada and her friends talk about boys during their sleepovers and not looking at those boys the same when we got back to school. Ms. Inthavong, our neighbor, with that grimy looking Bichon Frisé that growled at me when I walked around the neighborhood with Carter and Jackson. Spending the quarantine experimenting with different hobbies until I found one that stuck and using that to drown out Mama's incessant worrying about compromised immune systems and purifying the air.

"It was good," I say. I didn't have a perfect life in California. In fact, I ran away from my life there, but now, I kind of miss it. I'm kind of excited to go back.

"Is it true that it's more accepting?"

"Only in the big cities and even there it's—" I trail off, and Eric looks discouraged so I add, "Um...it can be easier to find...areas...for marginalized groups."

"You can say 'gay,'" he chuckles.

"Okay. There are places...some places there are whole neighborhoods filled with gay people. They can be a little racist, though," I add that caveat.

He rolls his eyes. "Black isn't safe. Gay isn't safe. I can't win."

"Sorry," I offer.

"It's not your fault." He shrugs. "Do you ever think of going back?"

I almost choke on my pizza when he asks. As I'm chewing, Naima walks up, and I know this is God wanting me to come clean.

"What y'all talking about?" she asks, standing next to me.

"Nosy," Eric teases. "I just asked if he wants to go back to California."

Now Naima looks at me, her doe-eyes wide and waiting for an answer. I swallow.

"You haven't been back this summer," she says in her soft tone. It's more an observation than a question, but I'm backed into a corner nonetheless.

"Yeah, um," I clear my throat thinking of how to phrase it. "I was waiting til you went to college and then I'll go back and see my family."

She nods and seems satisfied with that answer. That's the closest I've gotten to telling her the truth all summer and even still there's so much left out like when I leave, I won't be back. My parting gift to you will be a broken heart. I'm sorry Naima. I love you, but this is goodbye.

I finish the pizza then suggest, "Y'all want to finish the game?"

Everyone agrees so we all work our way down to the double blank domino. It's after ten when we finish, and Naima helps me pack the games in the car. She keeps rubbing her eyes and yawning.

"Thanks for doing this," she says. We're standing by the driver's side of the door. I wonder if I wrap my hands around her waist, will she recoil or will she let me? I decide not to push it.

"Yeah. I had fun."

"Me, too." Her hands are behind her back, and she sways on her tip-toes.

"Is it okay if I kiss you?" I ask. I know. I'm a desperate man.

"Why wouldn't it be okay?" she giggles.

Because I want to savor it, I wrap my arms around her and pull her close to me. With my hand cupping her face, I bring her lips to mine and slowly kiss her. When I stop, I whisper, "I love you."

"I know," she says before leaning her head against mine.

I close my eyes while holding her under the street light, breathing in her vanilla scent, listening to the cicadas and crickets chirp around us in the humid night, hoping to commit as much of this as I can to memory.

CHAPTER THIRTY-THREE
Naima

SAM: Nai I need your help

With Nell

Is she okay?

Is she sick?

She's fine. I wanted to go to Madison and pick up something for her can you ride with me

Do I have to?

It's a long drive.

Ill buy you dinner

You were gonna do that anyway

Tomorrow then?

Chapter Thirty-Four
Naima

It's drizzling when Sam picks me up. The window defogger makes the Jeep nice and cozy when I slink into the passenger seat. His old country music playlist serves as an accompaniment to the wheels splashing in puddles.

"What are we getting in Madison?" I ask, watching the green trees and gray sky blur past the window.

"She needs a cat tower. There wasn't a good one at Walmart," he says.

"Needs?" I lift an eyebrow.

The corner of his mouth tilts. "Yes, need. I was watching a video about stuff to make cats more comfortable. I got most of it, but I want her to have a good tower."

"You're taking this cat parenting thing serious?"

"Damn. Am I a cat dad now? I'm only eighteen."

"You're old enough to be a real dad. Remember Emma and Noah? Emma got pregnant junior year. Noah's like nineteen with a two year old."

"Yeah, but a real baby is different than a cat. I can leave Nell home alone."

"That's a good point."

"She did stand on me and yell every morning at six to feed her until I got her an automatic feeder. Maybe she is a baby."

"She's like what? Four now and she still communicates through screaming? I think you have it worse than parents." I grin.

"Yeah, so much worse," he smirks.

Gazing out the window, I smile thinking about how much I miss this. It's been about two weeks since I've seen him face to face. He's either with Dixie, Darius, or Marcus or I've been too exhausted from crying to see him, but today feels like one of the first regular days in a while. I'm glad.

"How are things with Kamron?" he asks.

"I apologized." I inhale then exhale slowly. I've never really talked about this stuff with Sam before because I always had Luna, and she knows what it's like to date boys. In a panic, I texted Sam because I had to ask someone for help, but maybe it would be better to have a male perspective on things.

"I don't know. I feel like...like he hates me or something," I explain. "He came by the other day for a game night. It was fun, but everything was still...awkward between us."

"I didn't get invited to a game night."

"You were out with your whores."

He snort-laughs, but then his face turns more serious. "He doesn't hate you."

I bite my lip before saying, "I know that logically. It's just—everything between us has been so easy, and this is like the first time something bad has happened and it's my fault—like it always is. I apologized, but it doesn't feel like it's enough."

For me personally, I need so many apologies to believe it. I remember when we were little and teachers used to force us to say sorry even when we didn't mean it. People love the appearance of an apology without the actual reparation.

"If he accepted your apology, I'd leave it at that, Nai. Don't overthink it."

I lean my head against the headrest and sigh. Maybe Sam is right.

"How are things with Dixie?" I ask since he knows all of my and Kamron's business.

"Good. She's moving at the end of this month."

She?

"Without you?" I ask.

"Without me."

Taken aback, I lift my eyebrows. I'm not sure if it's appropriate to celebrate that one, Sam isn't leaving me, and two, he's separating from the clout-chaser, Dixie.

"Are you okay with that decision?" I settle on saying.

"Yeah." He nods. "It was my decision, and I got a new cat I

have to take care of now. Thanks for that."

"You could've said no," I remind him.

"Neither of you would let me."

"Cat parenthood suits you." I smile at him, and he briefly takes his eye off the road to return the smile.

An hour later, when we get to the pet store in Madison, the brightness of the lights assault me. I inhale slowly and deeply then exhale just as slowly. *I can do this*, I remind myself. I grab a buggy and lean on it following Sam around the store. We head straight to the cat section, starting with the food. He's picking up packs of wet food trying to decipher which one would be best for Nell then he asks me.

"I don't know." I shrug and then point to the one with the prettier packaging.

The smell of wet dog hair and bird poop hang in the air, and I'm trying my best to breathe through it. Sam is taking his sweet time putting things in the buggy. When we get to the toy section, he shakes the toy or squeezes it to test it out. I work on breathing through the sensory circus going on around us. Towards the end of the aisle, he picks up a cat tunnel.

"Do you think she'll like this?" he asks.

"Sure," I say, hoping that agreeing with him will rush him along.

He tosses it in the buggy and then we turn. There's a glass window with kitties inside the kennels.

"Can we go in there?" I ask.

"We have a cat at home."

I let go of the buggy and open the door. Their litter box and dry food commingle into a smelly blend, but I power through it to see their little faces. Most of them are curled into a ball asleep, but one, a gray tabby, looks up at me through the grates. I slide my finger in there, and the tabby rubs its face against it. I want to take it home with me.

Sam walks in. "Nai, what are you doing?"

The paper attached to the grate says that her name is Bunny, and she's two. She's been in the shelter for the past six weeks. When I look up at Sam, he immediately shakes his head. "Nai, you can't."

"But look at her."

We do. Right then, a white girl bursts through the door with her mother. The daughter is pointing at the kitties, and the mother looks at me and Sam, frowns, then grabs her daughter and rushes out the door. I gaze out the window and see another elderly couple give me and Sam the stink eye. Sam is petting Bunny with his finger, oblivious to the hate directed at us. Is this what I've been oblivious to as well? That when me and Sam are together all people can think about is that we can't be friends? We're too different to be in this close proximity to each other. A Black girl and a white boy. Apparently, this kind of coupling was only okay during slavery when Black girls didn't have a choice, and white men could do whatever they wanted to with us.

Silly me. I thought I was just going to have to fight the pet store, but instead I get knocked down with racism. So much for having a good day.

"Can I get the keys?" I hold my hand out to Sam.

He looks at me bewildered. "What? No. Nai, you can't leave. We're not done."

"Please," I say. My voice cracks against my will.

He places his hands on my shoulders, and I flinch, afraid that this will direct more people's hatred in our direction. "Is it the lights?"

"And the smells and the noise and...everything." I wave my hands around gesturing to the many white people with squinty eyes and tight lips, angry that me and Sam are breathing the same air.

"Yeah sure." Sam reaches into his pants and pulls out the fob. "I'll try to hurry up."

"Thanks." I smile weakly and rush out the door.

The damp fresh air is a temporary relief because the drizzle has escalated to a downpour, and now I have to fight the rain back to the Jeep. I pull the rain jacket tighter over my hair and run to the Jeep, crawling into the back seat, pulling my knees into my chest and breathing. In through my nose. Out through my mouth. I'm just so overcome with feeling that I want to fight. The store. The people. The rain. Everything. But I'm so tired, and it's only little ole me. Instead I let my eyes slowly fill with tears and fall down the side of my face. When the tears tickle my chin, I wipe them away.

I stay in the backseat, curled up in the fetal position, looking out the windshield until Sam returns. Only then do I climb into the passenger seat and put on my seat belt. He doesn't ask if I'm okay. He already knows the answer. Instead, he reaches over the console and squeezes my hand.

"There's a Raising Cane's over there if you want something."

Raising Cane's is a luxury considering that this is the closest one to where we live.

"I'm not hungry," I sigh.

I just want to go home, bury myself in blankets, and cry.

He smooshes his lips together, starts the Jeep, and drives over to the Raising Cane's. He orders the four chicken finger basket swapping the coleslaw for extra fries and getting a sweet tea. When the cashier asks if he wants anything else, he orders a three finger basket with a lemonade. I know it's for me even though I don't want it.

He pays the cashier and grabs our drinks. Sipping the lemonade, it's the perfect mix of sweet and tart. When they hand Sam the bag, the smell of fried greasy food fills the car and my nostrils. My stomach responds immediately. Okay, maybe I am a little hungry.

He parks in the parking lot, and we eat to the soundtrack of the pouring rain, windshield wipers, and country music. Once we're on the road back home, I watch the city turn to trees and listen to the wind hum pass the Jeep. At some point, I take a nap and wake up to the headlights being on in the drizzling rain.

"Where are we?" I ask, not making out anything in the darkness surrounding us.

"The outskirts of RBS," he says.

That's probably another twenty minutes until we get home. I shift in my seat and breathe.

"Thank you for feeding me."

"You always get cranky when you're hungry." He smirks.

As much as I want to bite back, I smile instead. I'm grateful that he's staying here with me a little bit longer. Redbud Springs come into view, and I anticipate the next few sights. There's three traffic lights until we're out of city limits and then ten minutes until we're back at the house. Having eaten and napped, I don't feel the need to rush into bed anymore. Instead, I listen to the music playing which is country yes, but it blends seamlessly into hip-hop and pop.

"Who is this?" I ask.

"You like it?" Sam asks instead of answering my question.

"Yeah." It's country music but better because it's actually good.

"Tanner Adell. We can play her whole album if you want."

He reaches for his phone to play it, but I grab it instead.

"I got it."

The song is "Buckle Bunny." I click the deluxe album and

play it from the top. We make it halfway through. Each song sounds so different from the last. I finish "Bake It" before I get out of the Jeep.

"Thanks for coming today," Sam says. "I'm sorry I messed up your autism."

I snort. Like that's even possible. "The nap fixed every-thing."

"See you later," he says, putting the car in reverse.

I wave and shut the door, walking back into the house and putting this horrid day to an end.

Chapter Thirty-Five

Kamron

Naima's going to college is a constant countdown in my head. Twenty-nine days. I haven't been able to read, throw, watch TV, anything, and it's agonizing. I'm trying to respect the fact that she needs space to grieve Luna, that she only wants to meet once a week, that she gets too overwhelmed to text. I'm trying to be patient and wait, but I know everything is going to end soon, and I want to spend these last twenty-nine days with her. It seems that every time I try to talk with her, to spend time with her, it's like walking on a landmine. She's waiting to explode.

I video call her instead. She may not pick up. That's okay, at least I tried. The phone rings for a while. Right when I'm about to hang up, her face fills the screen. She waves. The room is dark except for her lamp. Her hair is covered in a bonnet, and an eye mask rests on top.

"You just wake up?" I ask.

She shakes her head no. "I haven't been out of bed today."

"Oh." I sit back in the armchair in my studio. It's a little after noon. I know that she may take longer than usual to get over a loss, but it's been almost three weeks.

"You remember our once a week deal?"

"Yeah," she says, then bites her lips and averts her gaze. "Is it okay if we skip this week? I went out with Sam yesterday, and it took a lot out of me."

"You went out with Sam?" I didn't mean to say that out loud, but it slipped. She can see *him*, but not *me*? *Her boyfriend*?

"Yeah. We got some stuff for Nell, and everything happened so fast." She wraps the blanket tighter around her body. "It stank and was loud, and there were these white people staring at us. I hated it. I felt so gross and—" She turns her face away. "I just need some time."

How can I argue with that? I can't ask her to be someone she's not even if I want her to be right now.

"Okay," I say.

She turns her attention back to the screen. "Thank you for calling me, though. I appreciate it."

"Yeah. No problem."

"Um" —she bites her bottom lip— "I'm gonna go."

"Okay."

She waves, and as her face leaves the screen, I slam the phone against the table.

"Fuck!"

My leg bounces. She doesn't want to see me because she was out with Sam? I want to see her, hold her, touch her, kiss her, but she wants to be with fucking Sam? And of course, he wants to be with her.

I look at the dried up clay and grab a chunk to wedge it, pushing it harder and harder into the table. When it struggles to give, I glance around the room and find a sack that I shove the clay in and smack it on the table. I slam and slam and slam the clay until Amaya shouts my name. I stop, and she's staring at me from the doorway.

"What?" I scream.

"Who you yelling at like that?" She crosses her arms.

"Sorry."

My chest rises then falls, and her face softens. "You have to tell her."

"I know. I—" A tear drops on my cheek. I quickly wipe it away.

"It'll keep eating away at you if you don't."

"I know," I nod. "I'll tell her."

Chapter Thirty-Six

Naima

Sam texted me early this morning to see if I was free today. Except for my daily agenda of crying, doom scrolling, and emotionally spiraling, I'm not too busy. Around six, he asks me to come over. As I'm walking to the door, he looks up from his phone and bong.

"Hey," he coughs, and I wave.

He shuffles getting up to open the screen door, letting me pass through. Nell runs out of Ms. Tish's room screaming, so I pick her up and swaddle her like the baby she is.

"Hola, bebita." She purrs into the crook of my arm. I stroke her silky fur and turn back to Sam who's putting his paraphernalia up. The smell of sweet sticky greasy food hangs in the air. I sniff trying to follow the scent when Sam says, "You ate?"

I shake my head no. "You wanted me over here for dinner?"

He walks over to the coffee table where brown packages of food are and plops on the couch. "I'm sorry for the other day.

I should've known better, but I wanted your help. This is my apology." He gestures at the food.

As I sit beside him on the couch, Nell jumps out of my hands and walks over to the cat tower that Sam assembled. I open one of the packages and pull out a Styrofoam box. Pork belly bao.

"Food is the best apology," I say even though I wasn't mad at Sam in particular, just the whole situation.

He grins at me.

"What'd you get?" I ask while grabbing more boxes out of the bag.

"Street food. Like on *DancingBacons*," he says and then turns on the TV and searches for their YouTube channel to play while I keep looking in the bag.

"Boba!" I yell once I open the bag with two boba teas in it. "God, I love you."

"Was boba all it took?" he jokes.

"Where'd you get all this stuff?"

Our little Chinese restaurant doesn't even serve half of this. He'd have to drive to Ridgeland or somewhere at least an hour away to get it.

"Don't worry about it." He points to a box with an X on it. "That's mine."

"You get one all to yourself?"

"It has octopus in it."

"Yeah. You can have that."

I've never had octopus, but if it's anything like shrimp, mussels, clams, and crab, I do *not* want it.

We sit back and try the different foods. Bbq buns. Taiwanese popcorn chicken. Sesame balls. Korean-style ribs. Fried gyoza. Japanese Fried Milk. With each thing I like, I nod enthusiastically at Sam like the mystery woman in the *DancingBacons* videos does. With each thing I don't like, I spit it out in a paper towel and pretend it doesn't exist.

While we're eating, he has his phone in his lap watching a baseball game with the volume on max. The noise of that is competing with the noise of the TV, and I can't focus on either one.

"Sam," I groan with half a dumpling in my mouth.

"What?" He looks at me, and I look at his phone. Sam is not Sam without multiple forms of stimulation. I get that. It's great for him, but it's the same thing that makes my skin crawl. How we've managed to get along all these years remains a mystery to me.

"Oh, sorry," he says and mutes his phone.

I lean over and look at his screen. It's players in blue, red, and white uniforms. "Is Shohei Ohtani there?"

He jerks his head towards me, and his eyebrows knit together. "How do you know that name?"

"Do you know him?"

"Yeah *I* do. How do *you*?"

I grin. "It's cause baseball is everywhere. I'm basically an expert by now. I bet I know more about baseball than you."

He smirks then shakes his head. "I doubt it."

Once we've put a dent in the food, we sit back, watch the sights, and listen to the sounds of southeast Asia. In this video, *DancingBacons* is reviewing a vending machine that makes a smoothie from frozen ingredients. We're both entranced by ingredients dispensing into the cup, the liquid being added, and then it mixing in the small window of the vending machine. After a few minutes, the smoothie is done for the man to review.

Chewing on a tapioca ball, I ask, "Why can't we have nice things like that?"

"I don't know," Sam shrugs. "People may try to steal it?"

"Steal a vending machine?" I ask. That's a bit extreme. "Why do we always go to the worst thing? Why can't we all have vending machines that can make us decent food instead of relying on fast food and junk?"

"Where would it even go?"

"Schools. Hospitals. The town square."

"The town square?"

"I don't know," I shrug. "Just thinking of options. I mean we have to travel so far already for this." I wave my hand over the coffee table of food.

"Well, you'll be right there in Jackson soon. Are you ready?" he asks.

I sigh. Am I ready? I've been so wrapped up in my grief over losing Luna that I haven't thought much about school.

"I wrote a list of things I'll need, but I haven't started packing. I'm kinda not ready to start a life where I'll know no one."

"I can come visit if that's allowed."

I don't know why I never thought about that before. "You'd do that for me?"

"Yeah, Nai," he chuckles. "I can visit you every once in a while."

I squeeze him and lay my head on his shoulder. He wraps his other arm around me as he lays his head on top of mine. I hold him for a good minute, grateful that he's always been and will always be with me.

"Just let me know if you need help with anything," Sam offers.

I finally let him go and nod. "Okay. Idk the plan yet. I have to ask Mom, but I'll let you know."

My attention turns to my phone lighting up. It's Kamron, video calling me like I asked him too, but I forgot. My heart thumps as the screen flashes, but I watch it until it darkens then breathe a sigh of relief.

"Everything okay?" Sam asks.

"I—" I press my palm to my forehead and squeeze my eyes shut. "He wants me to be better so bad, but I'm not and every time I see him, I feel guilty about it."

"You can't keep ignoring him."

"I know," I sigh. "It's just—I'm spending time with you right now. I can call him back later."

Sam's pink eyes stare at me, like he knows I'm lying. I want to keep avoiding Kamron and his desires to make me feel better. I won't feel better until I'm better. Anything he does until then will just make me feel worse.

"Can we watch?" I gesture towards the TV.

Sam drops it, and we watch video after video of *Dancing-Bacons*. As the food digests, my head feels so heavy that I lean against Sam's shoulder to support it. He smells like a sweet blend of earthy smoke and fabric softener. My breathing slows until I hear snoring.

"Who's snoring?" I ask, my eyes still closed.

"You." Sam says softly, a slight teasing in his voice. "Come on. Let me walk you home."

I follow Sam out of the air-conditioned cocoon of his house into the thick swampy air outside. I loop my arm in his and lay on his shoulder, letting him lead the way since my eyes are wont to close. There's grass, gravel, and then wood letting me know that I've made it to my porch. I yawn rubbing my eyes to coax them open but fail. Instead, I wrap my arms around Sam.

"Thank you for tonight."

"Yeah." He drags his knuckles down my spine in slow broad strokes. "Good night."

"Night," I say, letting him go and walking upstairs to my bed.

CHAPTER THIRTY-SEVEN

Kamron

Tonight's the night that I tell Naima that I'm leaving. It's exactly three weeks until she starts college, and I feel like that's enough time to say our goodbyes and move on. We're meeting at Sam's house for a trivia night. Naima says it's for Dixie's going away party. She's moving to LA...without Sam because of course he isn't leaving.

When I knock on Sam's screen door, Naima is holding Luna's cat in her arms. Hesitantly, I open the door and walk in. My back is against the wall. I'm not saying I'm afraid of cats, but why do they have sharp claws and teeth that they stay trying to use against people? Cats are unpredictable so it's smart of me to keep my distance.

Naima, on the other hand, is babying this creature like it's not capable of unspeakable violence.

"Do you want to hold her?" she asks.

"No thanks." I place a hand between us to fend off the

creature. Like I knew of this cat, but I always found a way around her. Mainly by never going into Luna's house except in cases of emergencies.

"But she's a perfect angel. Una angelita perfecta." She swings the cat in her arms. "Y bonita y pequita."

She kisses it on its head, and it croaks in response. I shudder and inch myself towards the living room and away from it. Sitting on the couch, Sam walks out from the back and towards Naima. She hands the cat to him, and he reaches for the cat, dangling it in the air, before attempting to cradle it. The cat jumps out of his arms and towards the living room, towards me. I slide back into the couch and thankfully, it thwarts her. She jumps up on the tower in one fell-swoop.

"I don't know why she won't let me hold her," Sam says.

"You gotta perfect your holding stance."

She folds her arms in front of her in a swing and moves them back and forth. Sam tries to imitate her. He swings around and jerks when he sees me.

"Oh, hey man," he says.

"What's up?" I say.

"Dixie will be here in a minute. She's bringing snacks and stuff."

"It's her going away party. Shouldn't we have done that?" Naima asks.

Sam plops in the recliner. "She wanted to do it."

Naima sits next to me and places her hand on my thigh. It's

only then that I realize that I haven't even said hey to her. No hug. No kiss. I'm off my game today. I interlace my fingers with hers, and she smiles. It's small, a little sad, but it's there. I rub my thumb across her knuckles to remind her that I'm still here, and I still love her. She lays her head on my shoulder while Sam asks what we're playing today. Naima brought a trivia game in a box.

"I'm not good at trivia," Sam says.

"I know," Naima giggles.

Even though she's laying on me, holding my hand, I sigh knowing that this could all end today, and when it does, the first person she'll run to is Sam who'll happily take her in and who won't have a girlfriend anymore.

When Dixie pulls up, she honks the horn. Sam jumps up to help her bring in bags and bags of groceries.

"I got everything," Dixie says, walking in with a sheet cake. "Chips, dips, sandwiches, fruit, a veggie tray, desserts. Oh and pizza in the car. Could one of you get it?"

"I'll get it," I volunteer, but Sam pats me on the shoulder and says, "It's okay. I got it."

I look at his hand on my shoulder and then back up at him. Who told him he could touch me?

Naima glances at the food then towards me, and I'm thinking the same. Who is all this food for?

"This is a lot...for four people," Naima says.

Dixie smiles. "Oh, I know. I wanted to make sure everyone

ate, and I didn't know what people liked. Sam said there's certain things you can't have."

Naima gnaws her bottom lips and looks uncomfortable, maybe a little bit guilty. "Thanks."

Dixie starts pulling food and serving trays out of bags. After a quick rinse, she's plating the food on the trays and arranging them on the island to look aesthetic. Yep, that's definitely for a video. Sam has already put the pizza on the counter and now Dixie is videoing everything. She slow-pans over the cake which says, "Good luck with your new adventure, Dixie."

Okay, I can kind of see Naima and Luna's beef with her. She's vapid and cares a lot about her image, but she's not mean or anything. I mean she's good at bowling and remembered Naima's sensory issues. She's not a bad person.

Sam wraps his arm around Dixie's shoulders. "Got everything?" he asks, and she replies, "Yep."

"Are you...excited...about going to Los Angeles?" Naima asks with a strained smile on her face.

Dixie's face brightens. "I already have an agent. He's the best, and we're going next week to look at apartments. It's like a dream come true."

"You're looking at apartments?" Naima asks this question to Sam who shakes his head.

"No. Just Dixie."

"Yeah, I'm going with my parents."

Naima purses her lips together and nods. The silence starts

to get awkward so I interject, "Congrats, Dixie. My sister actually knows quite a few people in the industry. I can connect you if you want."

"Really?" Her eyes widen. "That's really sweet. Thank you, Kamron. Now remind me, your family is from California?"

"Yeah from Sacramento and the Bay area."

She hums. "Do you miss it?"

There's that question again.

"Sometimes," I say. "But there's a lot of reasons why I love being in Mississippi."

The number one reason is sitting at the kitchen island looking at me with her big brown eyes. I never thought I'd meet someone as dynamic and beautiful as she is. I don't know if I'll ever meet anyone else as amazing as her. I'm pretty sure that's impossible.

Dixie smiles sympathetically. We grab paper plates, pile them up with food, and sit around the coffee table. Dixie and Sam are in the chairs while Naima and I sit next to each other on the couch. After a few bites, Dixie asks what we're playing first. Naima grabs the trivia box on the table and picks it up for everyone to see. She explains the rules. We all start at fifty points, and every time someone misses a question, points are deducted until someone is down at zero. Then the highest score wins. It seems like a lot to keep up with four individual scores so I suggest we play as teams.

"I don't know," Naima says at the same time Dixie replies,

"Yes, please."

"The rules don't say how to play as teams."

"We can figure it out," I say, but Naima bites her lips, hesitantly. "Hey, we're partners. We got this, okay?"

She nods, looking down at her hands folded into her lap. She exhales then says, "Okay. I guess it's the two of us versus the two of you."

"We got this Samuel," Dixie says, pushing her chair closer to the recliner.

"Who's taking score?" Sam asks.

"I can." Naima gets up and grabs a pen and paper. She writes "NK" and "SD" on the paper, and then grabs the first card. "I guess I can go first so I can show y'all how to play."

Naima reads the questions on the card. Out of four questions, Sam and Dixie get one.

"We'll call this a practice round." Naima says, marking out the deducted points.

Sam grabs a card, and Dixie and him take turns reading the questions. We answer all of them right and high-five each other at the end.

"Maybe we should play another game?" Sam suggests.

"Nuh-uh," Naima says. "Practice round over. Time to lose."

She grabs another card, and we take turns reading. Again, Dixie and Sam struggle through it, losing twenty points in one round.

"You sure it's just fifty points?" Sam asks. "Kinda seem like y'all are cheating."

"Why is the game always rigged when I'm winning?" Naima asks.

"I thought trivia was supposed to be well-rounded with sports and stuff. This is just school stuff."

"Well usually when I play no one loses twenty points in one round," Naima mumbles.

"Okay." I spread my hands trying to play peacemaker. "It's just a game, y'all."

"Maybe we should split up teams. Girls against boys," Sam suggests.

"Why are you trying to split up my team? It'd really be me against Kamron."

"What are you saying?" he asks

"You're not really competition," she answers.

"Whoa, Naima," I scold. "Let's finish the game. Okay?"

Sam leans back against the recliner. "I'm just saying there are better games."

"This is why you weren't invited to game night."

"Naima!" I'm really failing at keeping this game moving along.

"No, he always does this. Whenever I win, he gets mad. He's such a sore loser. This is like Clue and Monopoly and Jumanji and Uno all over again." She ticks each game off with a finger as she says them.

Sam crosses his arms over his chest. "I think we should just play a new game."

Naima gestures over the coffee table. "There are no new games."

"We can play Codenames," Dixie suggests.

Naima massages her temple. "I don't know what that is."

"It's like Guess Who, and we can play on our phones." She dangles hers in the air.

"Fine," Naima exhales. "But for the sake of this game, Sam lost."

"Whatever," he mumbles.

Dixie explains the rules to us. There are two spymasters, one blue, one red, and they have to come up with a hint to help their team guess their words. There's an assassin card where if someone picks it, that team automatically loses. Naima is confused about how to play so I decide to be our team's spymaster with Dixie.

"I think I should sit by you since we're both spymasters. Do you want to switch, Naima?" Dixie asks.

Naima stares at me and then says, "Sure," through a strained smile. If Luna was still here, they'd have some choice words to say in Spanish.

Dixie sits beside me and then points to my screen reiterating the directions so I understand them better. Our team is blue, and I start trying to group as many blue cards as I can with a hint. In their first turn, Sam gets four of the red cards correct. We all stare at him shocked, but he shrugs. "What? I've played before."

Naima throws her hands in the air. "You just wanted a game you could win."

"Nobody likes losing."

"But you want me to lose?"

He grins then shrugs again. Naima shakes her head but continues playing. Even with my best efforts, we're left with three cards when Dixie and Sam wins.

"Sorry," I whisper to Naima as we switch places.

She places her hand on my arm and offers a small smile. "You did good."

Sam and Naima sit next to each other, and I don't know what I was thinking. They're thigh to thigh, practically up under each other. And the worst part is, they don't even notice how close they are. I forcibly unclench my jaw, shift in my seat, and breathe. It's just a game. Nothing to get upset over.

Then she leans over and whispers something in his ear. He chuckles while looking at her phone and nods. They've been arguing most of the night, but now they're cozy and intimate with each other?

A hint pops up on my phone: Tienanmen 2. Instantly I pick "square" and "China."

"How could anybody know that?" Sam asks.

"You can't say I'm cheating. I asked you about it." Naima says, wagging her finger at him.

"It's just a nerdy answer," Sam mumbles.

Most of Naima's hints are like that, hyperspecific in a way that she knows I know it. Like everything she's thinking of is tailor made for me. That's her signature. When she loves you, she has a way of making the world seem like it revolves around you. Like you are her sole and most important focus. Even as she's sitting beside and kiking next to Sam, she's thinking of me.

Despite her excellent clues, we lose. This time we had one clue left, when Dixie correctly guessed the last clue.

"Wanna play again?" Sam asks.

Naima rolls her eyes. "You want me to lose again."

"That's the best part." Sam grins, and Naima shoves him.

Dixie picks up her plate and heads to the kitchen. "Anybody want cake?"

I follow Dixie to the kitchen to grab a piece for me and Naima when Naima yelps. I turn around, and she's flicking her hand near the cat who's sitting on her tower. Sam rushes to the kitchen, and I run to her.

"What happened?"

She pulls her hand out to me, and there's a fresh scratch from the demon cat. It's bleeding. Sam comes back with a paper towel, and I press it into the wound.

"Are you okay?" I ask.

She nods. "She does this when I get too close to her."

I glare at the cat who's curled into a ball with its eyes shut. It doesn't even care.

"It's fine," Naima says, "She scratches me all the time."

She turns her hands over to show me the scratches lining her arms. On her other palm is a relatively fresh scratch that's scabbed over. When I touch it, she winces. It's new, but it didn't happen today. So while I've been patiently waiting to see Naima, she's been here with Sam getting scratched up by this cat? My jaw tightens. My teeth clench. Looking up at her, she's still staring at her hand. Either she doesn't know that I know, or she doesn't care.

"Cake?" Dixie asks with two plates in her hand.

I'm still holding Naima's palm so she uses her other one to grab it.

"I'm good." I tell her. I'm already sick thinking of Sam and Naima. Together. Every single day that I waited by the phone she was here. With him. I got a video call, and he got her.

"Okay," Dixie says chipperly. "Y'all ready to play the next game?"

I should say no. I'm ready to go, but that just leaves her with him for longer.

"Yeah," I nod to Dixie. "I'm ready."

Naima nods, too, so we gather in the living room. Dixie wants to play the newlywed game since we're both couples.

"We can use questions online, but I think it's more fun to make our own that way we can personalize them. Usually we play with a white board, but give me a sec—" Dixie walks out to her car and returns with four small rectangular chalkboards and some chalk. She's prepared for anything.

She passes them out to us and then continues. "Hmm, I wonder if we should do the Newlywed Game or How Well Do You Know Me?"

"What's the difference?" Sam asks.

"Well, How Well Do You Know Me means one person asks the questions and everyone else has to guess instead of it being just the couple."

"That sounds better," Sam says. "I think I'd win."

Annoyed, Naima rolls her eyes.

"Okay, well. I can go first," Dixie volunteers. She put the chalk to her lip to think then she asks, "Am I a morning or a night person? We can start pretty simple."

It's a fifty-fifty question so I guess "morning" and write it down. She seems like the kind to wake up at six a.m. and go for a run before starting her day. Once we all have finished writing, we show our boards and then Dixie reveals hers. Night. Only Sam got it right.

"She doesn't wake up til eleven a.m.," Sam replies.

"It's true," Dixie pipes. "Okay, who's next?"

Sam volunteers. "Who is my...favorite fictional character?"

Naima yelps and excitedly writes down the answer. All I know about Sam is that he likes anime. Bad, old anime so I think of *Naruto* and then the most boring character on there, Naruto himself. We turn our board around. Dixie picked Philomena Cunk, and Naima picked Don Draper. Sam revealed his answer: Don Draper. I didn't take him for someone who liked *Mad Men*.

"Philomena Cunk was a good guess," he tells Dixie.

Naima shakes her head. "I can't believe you got me to watch that entire series with you."

"It's a good show," he says.

"If you say so." She wipes her board. Now that it's her turn, she's staring up at the ceiling, thinking about her question. She blows her lips. "Why is it so hard to come up with something?"

"You can think about your favorite thing," Dixie suggests.

"Fine. What is my...favorite...color?" She grimaces. "Now I gotta think about that."

I remember Naima in layers and layers of green. When we first met, she had green-tipped locs. Her crocs are green. She has so many shades of green in her closet. It has to be green.

We flip and Naima wrote "Green." I'm the only one who got it right.

Now that it's my turn, I think of one of my favorites. "Who's my favorite sports team?"

"Is there a specific sport?" Sam asks.

"Baseball."

It's the Giants. Naima bites her lips and taps the chalk to her board before her mouth widens into an O. She scribbles the answer. Dixie and Sam are slower to write something down. When it's time to reveal, Dixie has a question mark. Sam wrote the LA Angels, and Naima wrote the Giants. We high-five each other. We got each other's questions right. We probably would've beat them in the Newlywed game.

Each turn, the person asks a question about themselves, and we answer it. Sam gets most of the questions Dixie asks. Naima gets most of Sam and my questions. And Sam and I are tied for getting Naima's questions. We decide the first to get ten correct answers win. Sam and I are at nine. Naima is at eight, and Dixie is at five.

Sam asks his question. "What is my favorite song?"

Something about the way Naima furiously scribbles hits me. Every question Sam asked has been like that. I know they've been friends for pretty much their entire lives, but the fact that they know each other so well, that they've been a part of every single moment in each other's lives. It makes it inevitable that with me and Dixie both going to California, the two of them will be together in some capacity.

When we reveal our boards, of course Naima gets it. She gets everything about him. Now Naima, Sam, and I are all tied at nine. One more correct answer, and one of us wins.

It's Naima's turn and she asks, "Who is my favorite member of Little Mix?"

She grins at me then at Sam. "It's a hard one but y'all have like a twenty five percent chance of getting it."

I know this. I know I do. I know there's a Black girl and a white one. One is biracial and one pretended to be biracial, but what are their names? Sam has already written something on his board which heats me up. My ears, my chest, my feet are all hot. My hands are sweaty as I'm thinking of this answer. Is it Leigh-Anne? Naima liked it when I played her song on the way to the water park, but is she her favorite? Hers is the only name I remember so I write that down. We all reveal our boards. Both Sam and Dixie wrote Jade, and I wrote Leigh-Anne.

"You know Little Mix?" Naima asks Dixie before revealing her board.

"I love *Glory Days*, and Jade's new stuff is really experimental," Dixie replies.

"Yeah, I was definitely taken back with 'Angel of My Dreams.' I had to listen to it six times to really get it."

"Hello? The answer?" Sam waves his hand to rush her along.

She sighs and flips her board around. "It's Jade."

Naima looks at me sympathetically as Sam yells, "Four for four. Let's go!"

I slam my board on the table, and Naima reaches for my thigh. "It's just a game."

"It's not a fucking game!"

Chapter Thirty-Eight

Kamron

Naima's beautiful brown eyes are filled with fear? Hurt? And it's all because of me. She stands up and backs away from me. I take a step towards her. Immediately, I know what I did was wrong. I shouldn't have yelled. I shouldn't have gotten so angry. But she runs away. Away from me.

"Naima, don't!" I call after her.

I'm about to follow her when Sam blocks me. His palm is against the front of my shoulder. "You should go."

My teeth clench while I stare at him. He's gonna go after her and comfort her, and he'll do it over and over again long after I'm gone. I snatch my shoulder from under his grasp and walk to my car. Inside, I hold my head. I've never yelled at Naima. Never. Even if I'm frustrated or upset, I've never taken it out on her. She doesn't deserve that. She didn't deserve this. Looking across the yard at her house, her room light flashes on then off. I could go over there and apologize. Would she accept it or would she yell at me to leave her alone? Would she say she doesn't want to see me again?

In three weeks, she'll have her wish.

I slam my fist against the steering wheel. It wasn't supposed to be like this. I was supposed to tell her that I'm leaving and have three weeks left with her. Now, who knows if she'll ever see me again? Who knows if *she'll* break up with *me*?

I start the car to head home. My chest tightens with every thought that she'll leave me, that our relationship is over. When I get home, I unlock the door, and Amaya is sitting on the couch.

"What's up, Nephew?" she asks. Maybe the fear and anxiety is written all over my face, because she asks again, panicked. "Nephew?"

My legs walk me over to where Amaya is sitting, and I wrap my arms around her and bury myself into her shoulders. She rubs my back while the tears choke me. My face overheats. I didn't want it to end this way. I never want her to be mad at or afraid of me. I ruined everything.

CHAPTER THIRTY-NINE

Kamron

Naima, I know you don't want to speak to me right now and you don't have to. I'm really sorry for yelling at you. You didn't deserve that. You deserve an in-person apology, and I'll wait until you're ready for me to give it to you.

Chapter Forty

Naima

Kamron yelled at me.

He's never so much as raised his voice at me. He's always been the same patient and gentle boy I've known. I don't think I've ever even seen him frustrated. Now that I'm thinking about it maybe there were hints over the summer. Like sometimes his jaw would clench, but it'd quickly disappear. I thought I was seeing things. Maybe he was as upset as I was about Luna leaving, or maybe it was something else.

I keep replaying the night and wondering what caused him to get upset. We were playing games. We were losing...a lot. Sam was taunting us, but he always does that. I don't know what was different.

He didn't kiss me.

He always kisses me either when he sees me or before he leaves. He kisses me on the cheeks or my lips or my knuckles, but he didn't kiss me. I don't even think he hugged me. Nope, he held my hand after Nell scratched me. I rub the scratch on the side of my hand. That may have been the only time he touched me.

I grab my phone and open the text Kamron sent a few days ago. He sent it around midnight the same night. I wasn't angry at him, just shocked. I didn't think he was capable of losing his cool.

Even now, I'm not angry, but I am worried. It's August now, and I saw Kamron maybe five times during the entire month of July. I keep thinking that he's going to break up with me. That if I don't get better, if I'm not happier, then he's going to leave me. Still, it's not enough for me to text him back. To tell him to come over. To say that I want to see him again. Tears fill my eyes, and I sniffle. Of course, I don't want Kamron to break up with me. I love him, but I can't force myself to tell him. I can only sit in bed, stare at his text, and weep.

CHAPTER FORTY-ONE
Naima

Maybe I woke up on the right side of the bed this morning. My stomach growled so I went downstairs, ate two bowls of cereal, before deciding to tackle my room. Opening my windows, I yank the sheets off my bed and throw them over the staircase to the first floor to wash. I gather my clothes off the floor, dresser, and bed, sort them and bring the hamper down and start the wash. Then, I tackle my hair. It's been in two flat twists ever since I've taken down the braids Jada did. As the water heats, I undo them, shampoo, deep condition, fight the month's worth of tangles, and then rinse it out. With foam in my hair, I redo the twists and let it air dry while I sort my room.

Consulting the list I made, all I need to do is pack my clothes, my bathroom, and a few plants for college. Mom already bought bedding, towels, and decor specifically for my dorm room. Considering this is the first time I've gotten out of bed and done manual labor in several weeks, I decide to save it. Move-in day isn't for another ten days. Instead, I walk downstairs and outside where the thick heat slaps me in the face. I turn the porch fan on, and as I round the corner, Sam is sitting there on the edge of the wrap-around porch.

Leaning back on his palms, he looks up at me. "You're up."

"What are you doing here?" I sit beside him, but he returns his attention to the trees on the outer edges of our yard.

"Your mom asked for my help with something."

I sit down beside him. "She has two other boys in the house, and she asks you?"

"What can I say? I'm her favorite." A small smile tugs his lips.

"So...what's up?" I playfully knock my shoulder into his.

He stares out at the yard and rocks slightly. "Dixie left."

"Oh." I nod my head with my lips smooshed together trying to hide my smile.

"I know you hated her, but—"

"I didn't hate her," I interjected. "She was just—" Now I pause and look at him wondering if he can handle it.

"She was what?" he asks.

"She was using you."

He nods. "She was."

I stare at him, but the corner of his mouth tilts into a smile.

"You knew?"

"It was my idea."

I'm trying to figure out the math on that one when he explains. "Do you remember Ji-hoon, Marcus's cousin?"

I nod.

"That's Dixie's boyfriend. Ex-boyfriend, now I guess. Her parents didn't want them dating so we pretended to date. She helped me with sponsors. I helped her with her following, and she got to keep dating Ji-hoon."

I snort with disbelief. I was wondering why Sam dated someone like her, and he didn't. He wouldn't. That makes sense to me. I wish Luna was here so I could tell her that I was right.

"Why didn't you tell me?" I ask.

"You can't keep a secret."

"Shut up." I playfully shove him. "I can."

"What was your first thought when I told you?"

"I was right."

He chuckles. "Okay. Your second?"

"I gotta tell Luna."

He tsks. "Can't have everybody believing Dixie's my girl-friend if you're going around telling people she's not."

"It'd just be Luna," I say.

He shakes his head and grins, but slowly the grin fades and his eyes soften. He stares at me, and I know what he wants to say before he says it. "How have you—" he pauses then starts again. "Have you heard from Luna?"

There it is. Every time I hear her name it's like someone

snatches my heart out of my chest, cracks it open, and bares it to the sun.

"No," I swallow. "I haven't heard from her since we video-called."

I don't want to intrude because this is huge for her—going back to the country she was born in and seeing her family that she hasn't seen in eight years. Who am I to take that away because I want to see her and talk to her every single day? I want to hug her and hold her hand and fall asleep watching funny videos. I want to experience her and love her forever.

Sam stares at me. His jaw hardens, and he opens his palm waiting for me. When I grab it, he squeezes my hand and says, "I'm sorry."

"It's not your fault."

I wipe the tear that came outta nowhere away from my chin and try to smile to comfort him. To show him that I will be okay. He doesn't believe me. His lips are still smooshed together. I exhale. My shoulders slump, and my hands fold into my thighs. He rubs my back, his knuckles dragging along my spine, as I breathe in the warm morning air and breathe it out. For weeks I've been trying to place this feeling—the feeling that I'm exposed and raw at the same time.

"I'm heartbroken," I confess.

Sam offers a sympathetic smile and places his hand on my knee. I lean all the way back on the porch and stare up at the ceiling.

"I understand now how people can die of a broken heart. Friendship is the greatest love of all."

Friendship isn't bogged down with sexual feelings and good looks. I mean, Luna's hot, but it's more than that. She loves me for who I am. I love her for who she is. There's no ulterior motives, just love laid bare.

"I don't think you'd be doing all this if I left," Sam says.

"I would still miss you. A lot." I say. He's right. I may have known him longer, but Luna is different. She's the light of my life.

He knocks his elbow into my side. "Yeah I couldn't leave you and my mom. And with Nell, you made sure I couldn't leave."

"How is she?" I ask.

"All she wants is treats, naps, and pets. She's just like you."

I smile because of course she is.

"Thank you for taking care of her. If it wasn't for you she could be in a shelter or dead."

"I don't think she'd die."

"The shelter kills," I explain. "And people don't like black cats simply because they're black. You saved her life."

"Shit. People don't like black cats?"

"Racism is a disease or in this case fur-ism?"

He laughs, and I join him, and it feels good to share this moment together. This easy, fun moment. For the past month, Sam has been a reprieve from all the grief that's been flooding me. I'm grateful so I wrap my arms around him and hug him.

He's hesitant at first, but then he wraps his arm around me.

"Everything okay?" he asks.

"Thank you," I mumble into this shirt. "For everything. You have been...a balm these last few weeks."

I break the hug and wonder if he understands what I'm saying. I appreciate him giving me the space to be heartbroken, making me laugh, distracting me with Nell. I appreciate him accepting the ugly parts of me because I needed that. I needed to feel normal again.

"I wouldn't be doing my job as your best friend if I wasn't."

He has a point.

"Well, you've done a great job."

"I know." The corner of his lips quirks in amusement, and it forces my smile.

"I'm glad you exist."

He squints as his eyes look over me, puzzled. I guess it's a funny way of saying that I love him, and I'm glad that he's my best friend and that I get to spend my life with him. When he doesn't say anything, I ask. "Are you glad I exist?"

He chuckles, "Nai."

"Are you gonna say it back?"

"I'm glad you exist." He rolls his eyes while saying it.

"Yay!" I clap and then wrap my arms around him again. "That's all I ever wanted to hear."

"I'm sure you've wanted other things."

"Right now," I say with my arms still wrapped around him.

"All I want is you."

He rubs my arm but looks out towards the edge of the yard.

"Have you decided what you're going to do now?" I ask.

"I'm...going back to school."

I stare at him. This was the guy who's asked on more than one occasion what's the point of school and why do we have to do it. He constantly said when he graduated, he was done.

Sam sees my face then explains, "Darius is doing the electrician program at Attala. He says if you go for a year, you can start working and make *money*."

"So you're gonna be rich?"

"It's stable. More stable than TikTok," he sighs. "I think I'm done making videos. I helped Dixie so now it's time to move on."

Wow. I guess we've all spent this summer growing up and deciding what's best for us. For Luna, it's moving back to Mexico. For Sam, it's quitting TikTok and going to trade school. For me, it's going to college to study biochemistry. We're all getting a little bit closer to our dreams, even if it's moving us farther away from each other.

"I'm proud of you," I say. I'm happy he's decided a path that works for him.

"Thanks. How about you? You ready for college?"

I nod. "I think so. Mom's bought most of the stuff for my room. Just need to pack my clothes and stuff. You better come visit me."

"I will." He grins then he rubs his palms together. "You talked to Kamron yet?"

"No," I say, biting my bottom lip. "He apologized immediately. Told me to take my time getting back to him, but this has been the first day getting up and doing stuff. I need to put my clothes in the dryer, but yeah. I'm gonna talk to him."

"It's been a week."

"I know. I—this is gonna sound bad, but it's been nice. Not having to answer to him. Not having him linger over me wanting me to feel happier. Not having that pressure actually helped me, I think, but I do miss him."

He scoffs. "He looks at you like the heart-eye emoji. You should tell him sooner than later."

The heart-eye emoji. My brain offers flashes of Kamron's face. His beautiful smile. His long eyelashes. His bow-shaped lips. The way he looks at me like I'm the sun—the center of his universe. My thoughts shift to memories of laying in his arms, smelling the sandalwood and lavender emanating from the crook of his neck. My heart aches to see him again.

"I will," I promise Sam.

I glance down at the hands folded in my lap. I have to apologize to him. Maybe in my grief, I've been pushing him away, and he didn't deserve that. He deserves better, too.

Chapter Forty-Two

Kamron

Naima texted me that she was ready to talk this morning. I've spent the past two weeks sitting on the couch staring at my phone waiting for it to vibrate, talking to Peri about my apprenticeship, or packing up my stuff to ship off to California, but today it's time. I have to apologize and tell her the truth.

When I pull up to Naima's driveway, Sam is crossing the porch making his way down the ramp to walk to his house. I've been thinking a lot about him these past few days and how I might've overreacted to him having feelings for Naima. Feelings don't have to be acted on. They're just an option.

As I'm opening the door, he rushes behind the car, probably trying to avoid me. I can't blame him. I call after him anyway.

"Sam?"

He whips around to face me, and I swallow the rising betrayal in my throat.

"Can I talk to you?"

He puts his hands in his pockets, faces me, then nods.

"About the other day, I shouldn't have yelled. That was my bad. I uh…my parents, um, I'm moving back to California, and I've been worried about Naima. I was wondering if you could, um, can you make sure she's okay while I'm gone?"

That was the hardest sentence I've ever uttered in my life.

Naima is not mine. She's hers, and I want to make sure that wherever she is, she's safe, protected, and loved. As much as it hurts to admit, Sam can do that.

He stares at me, unblinking. His lips are drawn into a tight line, and his jaw flexes when he nods.

"Hey boys," Naima says, her voice melodic, as she walks towards us.

"I'm gonna go," Sam backs up and starts walking towards his house.

"What's that about?" Naima asks me. Her eyes searching from Sam's retreating form to my face for answers.

I cup her face with my hands like I've done so many times and have taken for granted, like I may be doing for the last time today. I watch her eyes flicking back and forth, looking down until she's comfortable enough to look back at me, and I just breathe.

"I'm sorry Naima. You didn't deserve me yelling at you."

"It's okay," she's quick to say.

"It's not." I lower my hand to reach for hers. "Can we sit

down?”

She nods, and I lead her to the porch. We sit on the swing, the swing where we had our first kiss, and I hold her hands, rubbing my thumbs over her knuckles.

“Is everything okay?” she asks hesitantly. I think even she knows what's about to happen.

“I wasn't being honest with you. I've been scared that if I told you the truth that you'd hate me, but I think it just made everything worse—”

“You're breaking up with me?”

“I'm moving back to California.”

We say the words at the same exact time, but the hurt in her eyes lets me know that the words have landed. There's an ache in my chest, and once tears start forming in my eyes, I clear my throat to try to push them away.

“I don't know if you remember the time you said you liked me at homecoming. I said I wouldn't be in Mississippi forever. At the time, I told my parents I'd only be here for a year, but then I got them to push it to two years and then for the rest of this summer, but it's time. I have to move back.”

Her face is stone. It's only her eyes that glisten more and more with each word that I say.

“When do you leave?” she whispers.

“I can stay until you go to college.”

She nods, staring down at our intertwined hands on the swing between us.

"I'm sorry, Naima."

She nods again, but when she lifts her head to look at me, I can see the paths the tears took down her cheeks and where they pool along her jawline. She stands up and starts walking towards the house, and I know that this is it. This is when she says she never wants to see me again.

Before she reaches the door, she turns back but continues looking at the ground when she asks, "Can you...can you stay here?"

"Yeah, I can."

"Okay," she says and rushes into the house.

I lean my head back and rock in the swing. She knows now and while I expected to feel dread, hurt, and sadness, I feel all of those, but I also feel relief. She knows the truth now, and there's nothing else that I have to hide from her. I don't have to pretend that it's okay when it's not.

To give her space, I lean against the swing and look out towards the end of her yard, past the garden that she shared with me almost two years ago, past the spot where we looked up at the stars and shared our second, third, and fourth kiss. I'll miss how green the trees are, how blue the sky is, and how white the clouds are. I'll miss how the air is generous with swampy heat but also comforting shade, how Mississippi is a state full of give and take. Most of all, I'll miss her.

After a few minutes, I walk inside and stand in the living room, looking up at her bedroom door. It's shut, but I can still hear the low wail coming from her room. It's my fault she's sad, but she wants me to stay here so I do. When my phone vibrates, and she's texting me to come up, I find her cocooned in the blankets on her bed so I join her. I wrap myself in its salty wet warmth and face her.

"Thank you for telling me," she says, her voice scratchy from crying.

"I'm sorry it took me so long."

Her thumb rubs my cheek, and she stares at my lips then up at me. She swallows, and I don't want to pressure her to give me something she doesn't want so I wait. Wait until she inches closer to me. Wait until her lips touch mine then I complete the kiss. I never realized a kiss can be sad, that it can be filled with hurt and sorrow, but when she breaks the kiss, I say, "I love you."

I want her to know this, even if she's too hurt to hear me right now. I want her to know that I love her, and I always will, forever, until I die. Nothing will ever change that.

Chapter Forty-Three
Naima

I f I'd known that by the end of the summer I'd lose my best friend and my boyfriend, I'd make different decisions about how I spent my time. I feel cheated that he waited so long to tell me. That I had less than a week left with him before I have to go college.

Right now, he's throwing on his wheel. Most of his studio is packed up. There are boxes in the hall full of his stuff. I guess we've both been getting ready to leave. He told me that he got an apprenticeship with this huge ceramist. It's bittersweet to know he's going to live out his dream, and I won't be there to support him.

I watch his hands steady and sure as the clay spins within them. His eyes are soft and lips are relaxed as he cones up then down, the clay molding to his hands. It was at that wheel that he asked me to be his girlfriend, and I very enthusiastically said yes. A few months after we started dating, he tried to teach me how to throw pottery. I made a plate. It was supposed to be a bowl, but I got so frustrated with the clay, frustrated that I wasn't able to pull the walls up, that I settled for a plate. Watching his steady, practiced hands, I know that he needs this, this centering of both the clay and himself.

He wraps the clay up and adds it to a packed box of his supplies. As he's driving me home, there's one question that bothers me. Why does this have to end? He's just moving. I don't understand why that means we have to break up.

Once he parks in the yard, he grabs my hand and rubs my knuckle. That's his signature. It's like tapping on the door and seeing who's home. Letting him kiss my hand is an answered door inviting him in to kiss me.

After he kisses my knuckles, I ask, "Why can't we try long distance?"

He looks at me and then out of the windshield. His eyebrows draw together with worry as he bites his bottom lip.

"It's not fair to you."

"What does that even mean?"

The heat rises in my chest because I think being fair is knowing all summer that he's leaving and telling me about it so I can be prepared. So I can say goodbye properly, not waste it crying in bed for a month.

"I mean," he sighs. "Once I leave, I don't know if I'm coming back, and I don't want you waiting on me...waiting on something I can't give you."

"So I'll never see you again?"

It's that possibility that does it. That makes it feel like my rapidly beating heart is about to explode. I may never see Kamron again.

"Maybe," he whispers.

I stare out the passenger window, and tears blur my vision.

"Okay," I say. I can't be angry at him. This is all the time I have left.

"I'm sorry."

I turn to him and watch his eyes glisten with tears. With my thumb, I wipe the corner of his eyes, and his lips turn up into a sad smile. I have never seen Kamron cry before, but the certainty that this is hurting him as much as it's hurting me comforts me. While I'm mad at him for not telling me, I can understand why it took so long. He doesn't want to say goodbye either.

I lean over the console and kiss him on the cheek, smiling softly before walking towards the house.

Luna calls. I think it's a mistake at first and stare at the screen for an ungodly amount of time before I click the answer button. Her very tanned face fills the screen.

"Hey, girl, what's up?"

I haven't heard her voice in so long that I want to cry.

"How are you?" I muster with a shaky smile.

She sighs. "Girl, Dad messed up our shipment. He said it would be two to three days, but it was *weeks*. We've been staying with family and friends waiting for our furniture and stuff to come in. We *just* moved in."

She leans back on her bed and holds the camera in the air. All this time I was worried that she had started a new life and was having so much fun that she forgot about me, but she was dealing with her own problems. It was nothing personal. I breathe a sigh of relief.

"I'm happy that you're safe and finally moved in," I say because it's true.

"I'm sorry it took so long to call," she apologizes.

"It's fine," I say.

"How's Nellie?" she asks.

I laugh because the last time I was with Nell, she yelled at me as soon as I opened the door, walked me to her food bowl, and screamed for me to feed her. When Sam came out of his room, he yelled at me because he had already fed her.

"It's Nell now. Sam changed her name."

Her eyebrows lift and eyes widen. I proceed to tell her everything she's missed. Sam is taking his role of cat dad very seriously. He started trade school with Darius a few days ago. Dixie was a fake girlfriend who's now moved onto Los Angeles. Luna jokes about Sam trying to turn his life into a romance novel. I tell her that I'm packed for college. We leave tomorrow night so we don't have to drive an hour and a half on move-in day. I'm nervous and excited about starting my biochemistry degree and meeting new people. I'm also sad. Sad about leaving Redbud Springs behind. Sad that Luna's in another country, and Kamron's moving two thousand miles away.

"How's Kamron?" Luna asks because she's noticed that I've not mentioned him.

I swallow and prepare myself for the truth. That I have two days left with him and I may never see him again.

"He's moving back to California." I fidget with my fingers when I hear her gasp. "We're breaking up."

"I'm so sorry, Naima."

"It's okay. I—"

"Hey," Luna calls my attention. "It's not okay."

"This is part of growing up, right?" My voice cracks. Everyone says growing up is letting go and moving on, but it hurts. It hurts so fucking much.

Luna's lips smooshes together, and her cheeks redden. "I wish I could hug you."

That sends me over the edge. She's not here. As nice as it is to talk to her, to see her face, I want to hold her and smell the coconut shampoo she uses and lay on her shoulder and have her lay her head on mine. I want to hold hands with her. I want to hug her.

An avalanche of tears cascade down my cheeks, and I can't stop them. Can't stop my throat from suffocating the sobs trying to escape. Can't stop the heat rising up from my chest, through my throat and to my cheeks. Can't stop anyone from leaving me or from all of us moving on with our lives. I can't stop growing up.

Through the screen, Luna looks as helpless as I feel, but she stays with me through the tears. I feel guilty that she had to watch me. I tried my best to hide the sadness from her, but I'm glad she's sitting with me, too.

"I love you," I tell her.

"I love you too, babe." Tears fill her eyes as well.

We stare at each other through the screen in our separate countries. I never would've known that when I met Luna she would mean this much to me, but I'm grateful, for whatever reason, she still wants to be my best friend. I'm grateful that she still loves me.

CHAPTER FORTY-FOUR
Naima

After Mom gets home from school, Sam helps me pack up her car with my stuff. He started trade school earlier this week. His classes are from nine to three so Nell barely even notices he's gone. When the car is packed, I squeeze Sam inhaling the smell of fabric softener and sweat.

"I'm going to miss you," I say, the words muffled into his neck.

"I'll come see you next weekend if you want me to."

"Really?" I ask, breaking away from him.

He rolls his eyes.

"I may surprise you and be a social butterfly and make so many new friends."

"I hope you do. Make new friends, I mean," he says.

"You want me to replace you?"

"No. I don't want you to be alone while you're there."

I lay my head against his neck and just hold him. I close my eyes and listen to the trees softly sway, the birds chirping about, and his heartbeat thumping. When he tries to break the hug, I hug him tighter. He chuckles, acquiesces, and then continues the hug.

"If we let go, I have to leave you," I admit.

"Hey." He pulls his head away to look at me. "I am so proud of you, Nai."

He rubs my back as he says it, dragging his knuckles up and down my spine, but it's something in the way his face softens that makes me believe him. That I'm someone worth being proud of.

"You ready?" Mom asks, walking down the stairs of the porch.

I squeeze Sam one last time before I have to leave. He dramatically grunts like I'm squeezing him too hard. Before I let go, I plant one last kiss on his cheek and get in the car with Mom. She rolls down the windows and reminds Sam, "Make sure Markese gets on the bus tomorrow, please."

Sam nods. "I will. Bye y'all. Drive safe."

I wave and watch as he gets smaller and smaller in the rearview mirror. When we get to the rental in Jackson, Kamron's already there. His car is packed to the brim with boxes and suitcases. His pottery wheel is on the passenger seat. Tomorrow, he starts his thirty-two hour cross country drive home.

Kamron meets me at the door, and we hug, a somber embrace. It's been like this since he's told me. Every hug, every kiss could be our last so I try to be as present for it as I can. I want to remember the sandalwood lavender soap he uses and the sweet curl cream he puts in his hair. His ragged breath as it shakes in my ear. When he pulls away, I search his face for the parts that I love: his hooded eyes, round cheeks, and bow lips. His wide nose, now pierced, just like mine. His everything.

"Hate to break y'all up, but I gotta sit down," Mom interrupts, and I realize that we've been blocking the door.

He chuckles. His mouth turns up into his perfect smile. The one that made my heart flip-flop years ago. The smile I used to think was all mine, but it never was. It was his, and he shared it with me for a while. Maybe that's all love is—a sharing of ourselves that we can retract at any time. Now is that time.

Since it's our last night together, Mom turns the other way when I decide to sleep in Kamron's room instead of my own. I lay on my back, staring up at the dark ceiling, my heart pumping too furiously to let me sleep. I'm nervous, excited, scared, and sad about tomorrow. My life starts in so many ways that I'm excited for, but that new beginning simultaneously means endings.

I look over to Kamron who's also not asleep even though it's getting later and later.

"Where are you driving to tomorrow?" I ask, hoping that the more I know, the less worried I'll be about him.

"I'm thinking Fort Worth," he says. "I don't like driving

more than eight hours a day."

So it'd take him at least four days to get home.

"Are you planning on stopping anywhere?" I twiddle my thumbs, trying to distract myself from what his road trip means.

"I went to Sequoia and the Grand Canyon when I drove down here. I was thinking about staying in Albuquerque on day two. I've never been, but it was a pretty city to drive through." He pauses. "How about you? Are you excited about tomorrow?"

"It's just move-in and welcome weekend," I tell him. "I have Intro to Cell Bio on Monday. Labs on Wednesdays."

I'm ecstatic about starting them both, and I try to hold onto this excitement. Because I'm a freshman, most of my schedule is core classes that everyone has to take.

Kamron chuckles. "It's been almost two years since we were lab partners."

"Yeah. Worst day of my life," I joke.

He laughs and then turns over to look at me. I face him. As he caresses my cheek, he whispers, "It changed my life."

Tears sting my eyes, and my chin wobbles. I know he feels this because he leans in and kisses me on my forehead. He wipes the tear that he knows has fallen, and he pulls me close to him. The heat of his body mixes with the heat building in my face, and I struggle to breathe, but he holds me throughout the night, and we wake up in each other's arms.

The morning of move-in the air is damp, still, and filled with the distant sound of sirens and cars. Mom drives through the gate and pulls into Olin Circle. Volunteers unpack our car and start carrying my stuff to my room. Kamron and Mom help me unpack. Thankfully, I don't have a roommate. The perks of being autistic, I guess.

Once everything is unpacked in my room, Mom decides that she wants to walk across campus. She gives me a look, like this is an excuse to leave me and Kamron alone, for me to say goodbye.

Kamron looks around the room, and my palms sweat. My heart races, but I focus on him.

"Everything looks good. It's a beautiful campus." He's looking out of my window to the courtyard below.

"Yeah," I say, offering nothing but a word to fill the silence.

"It seems like—"

And I kiss him. Just like our first kiss on the porch, so full of a desperate desire to make a moment last forever. To seal it with a kiss. I pin him against the wall, and his arms wrap around me, pushing me closer to him. I break away because I need to breathe, and he exhales.

"Please, don't forget me," I say. I know how desperate I sound, but I don't care.

"I could never forget you, Naima. I love you."

My head sinks. "I know."

"Can you say it back? Please."

It's the way his voice cracks on "please" that lifts my head up. Tears fill his eyes, and I reach to wipe them away.

"I love you, Kamron."

The kiss he stamps on my temple lingers. After this, he's going to get in the car headed for Sacramento. After this, I won't have a boyfriend. Maybe this is the hardest part of life—the people who come and go. Through death, moving, and breakups. Love doesn't leave just because people do, but they have a right to their own life, their own world, their own stories, and I can be grateful that I shared a little bit of it with them.

Right now as I hold Kamron as tightly as I can, as I inhale his cologne, his sorries, and his goodbye, I know I will one day be grateful for the opportunity to say goodbye to someone I love. I know that the love I have for him may always live on within me, and I know that an ending doesn't always mean the end.

Acknowledgements

Book Twos are always a roller-coaster for me to read in a serial series. It's where the protagonist ends on the lowest of their lows, but it's also where we see the characters shine because we're not bogged down by the worldbuilding.

This book was no exception.

It was emotionally heavy for me to write. It's no secret that these characters are inspired by real-life people from my past. (No, Naima is not a self-insert of me. Quit asking me that question) But, writing this book reminded me what these people brought to my life while also unearthing the grief from being separated from them by time and distance. Luna, Naima's best friend, is the love child of three of my teenage friends: Claudia Hernandez-Sanchez, Myeshia McDonald, and Carmen (McDaniel) Ervin. Luna is infused with different aspects of these three women, but I also see her as a separate entity. Creating Luna and the bond she shares with Naima helped me to remember, grieve, and honor the bonds I shared with these women.

Thank you Claudia, Myeshia, and Carmen for loving my weird undiagnosed ass and thinking I was beautifully and perfectly made even when I constantly panicked about something being "wrong" with me because of how hostile everyone else was towards me. Your message eventually stuck. I would not be where I am today without your love, support, and influence in my life. I am forever grateful that y'all exist.

As always, thank you Leah Nicole, for showing up for this book. Writing one book is hard. Writing several, even harder. This book was written when I received rejection after rejection for *About the Boy* because traditional publishing couldn't find a place for a main character who was Black *and* autistic *and* female. Thank you me for believing in this book and in this series and honoring our vision anyways.

Thank you to my ancestors, the ones who came before me, for believing in my right to exist, for protecting my vision, and for supporting my future. I literally would not be here without you. Thank you to my family for sharing with me the gift of storytelling.

Thank you to the many wonderful people who believe in me and supported my work financially when I needed help making this book a reality. God bless Akanksha Aurora, Amaris Ramey, Andrea Sexton Dumas, Anna Schwartz, Beverly Morrison, Christopher Cunningham, Dana Savell, Erin Becker Nordhof, Julia Mallory, Keri-Elizabeth Waites, my sissy, Kimberly Fleming, KJ Stone, Liz Allen, Michala Sullivan, Nancey B. Price, and Suzanne Glemot. Everybody thank them for this book being in your hands.

Thank you Govi for coming through with not one, but two covers. Working with you reminds me to not be too rigid about my vision, and it's always beautiful to see what we can create together.

I have to acknowledge Gunnar Boleen's contributions to this book. Years of being forced to watch the Pittsburgh Pirates lose gave me the baseball knowledge needed to write those scenes. At least something productive came from the prison of watching year-round sports.

And because a book is nothing without a reader to complete it, thank you, Reader, for trusting me to continue to tell this story. I hope it broke your heart a little bit, and I hope that you stay around for the next book so I can put it back together again. I do not take for granted that you are spending what precious time you have on this earth reading my words. Thank you for making my author dreams come true.

About the Author

Leah Nicole Whitcomb is a community storyteller from Mississippi who writes about Black folks, love, and magic. She co-hosts the award-winning Hoodoo Plant Mamas podcast. Her writing has been featured in *Sistories, Samjoko Magazine* and the young adult anthology, *All the Ways a Heart Burns.* A Courage to Write Grant recipient, Leah's work has been supported by The deGroot Foundation, Voices of Our Nation Arts Foundation, Bereket Writers, Women of Color Writers Podcast, and the Women's National Book Association. She is the author of the short story collection, *Apocalypse Still*, and the young adult romance, *About the Boy*.

Love Me or Leave Me

Book 3

"Mask!" I hand one to Sam.

I had mine on before we stepped inside the New Orleans airport, but Sam keeps coming up with excuses like, "Nobody else is wearing one."

"Okay *they* are fine breathing in everybody's air backwash and swapping germs and ruining their vacation. You really think people paid hundreds of dollars to go to Mexico, and they're just not gonna hop on a plane because they're sick? That person's probably sick now." I point to some rando across the aisle.

"Why did you say 'air backwash'?" he groans while making a show of pinching the metal nose piece and looping the straps behind his ears. His beard peeks out from the sides of the mask.

He huffs behind it, but I don't care. This is the first time that we're seeing Luna since she moved over two years ago. It's a momentous occasion, and I don't want to ruin our vacation with anybody else's germs.

Even though his face is masked, I can tell he's pouting while he's scrolling his phone. People are still filing into the plane so I check mine too before we have to set it on airplane mode. Opening Instagram, I flip through everyone's stories about finals. Thankfully this semester, I was able to finish my last two finals early so I could pack up and leave. Literally nothing could stop me from this trip. As I exit the story to scroll through my feed, his face pops up. It's been a while since I've seen him: Kamron.

He's wearing a black tee with blue jeans near a fountain with a fancy castle in the background. The location is tagged Madrid, Spain. It's the latest in his international adventures. I wonder who took the picture, what he ate, if he's having fun. I often wonder if he would've stayed in Mississippi, would I have kept him from traveling the world? Would I have stopped him from living his life?

"Everything okay?" Sam whispers near my ear.

I jump out of my trance, reorienting myself to the plane and Sam, his eyebrows drawing together with worry.

"Everything's fine."

I double click the picture and close the app, putting my phone on airplane mode. Kamron probably doesn't think about me anyway. I need to think about this trip and seeing Luna again.

When the flight attendants start their demonstrations, I interlock my fingers with Sam and lean on his shoulder while listening to them talk about how to use the oxygen masks. There's still five hours before we land in Mérida and then another hour and a half before we get to our rental in Celestún.

Sam wraps his arm around me. Even through the mask, I can still smell the fabric softener in his clothes. I cozy up to him while I wait for airplane snacks before taking a nap.

When I wake up and look at the screen, it says we have another hour and a half before we land. Sam's still asleep, snoring softly. I lift the window cover and stare out at the turquoise water. It's so beautiful, and there's so much of it. I smile knowing how badly I need this. This semester has been rough. I've heard so many horror stories about the difficulty of Organic Chem, and none of them accurately portrayed how horrifying it is. I was fighting for my life and ended up with a B. It's the lowest grade I've made since being at Millsaps, and that's before my final is added. What if I end up with a C? I may actually have a heart attack.

I lean back against the headrest of the seat, breathing in deeply and feeling my warm breath fill the mask. At least I got my internship next semester. That's honestly what's keeping me going at this point. Next semester, I'm working in a lab for the Mississippi Department of Environmental Quality. Only eight students were accepted, and I was one of them! I'm so much closer to living my dream, and maybe once I'm actually applying all of the things that I'm learning, everything will click for me. My dream will be realized.

Right now though, I'm just happy to take a breather, to be free from the shackles of classes, and to see my best friend in the whole world, Luna. Luna's bringing her partner, Ari. I've only seen the one picture Luna sent me when they went to a concert together. They wore coordinated outfits, and Ari kissed Luna on the cheek. I'm honestly so proud of her. I remember when she really struggled with coming out, and here she is with a whole partner!

By the time Sam wakes up, we have about thirty minutes until the plane lands. When it does and we deplane, we're welcomed into a bright, beige building with windows for walls. It's giving going out of business mall. I don't know why I thought it'd have more personality.

"Are you hungry?" Sam asks. "I'm starving."

He knows my hunger cues are nonexistent, but when I smell burgers and fries, my stomach perks up and leads me to a Johnny Rockets. They claim they made the original hamburger. I don't know anything about that, but we both order a burger, fries, and a vanilla malt. I order an extra water because I know Sam. He claims that milkshakes make him thirsty.

After eating, Sam asks, "How are we getting to Celestún?"

I roll my eyes. This boy really does rawdog life. I don't

understand how people can just expect everyone else around them to handle things.

"I booked a taxi." I check my phone. "It should be here in about fifteen minutes."

We walk to the front of the airport to sit while I check my booking for the taxi number and am shocked to see it right in front of me. As I head towards the taxi, the driver pulls down the window. He doesn't look much older than us. Twenty-five, maybe. I confirm that he's our taxi, and Sam and I put our suitcases and bags in the trunk before shuffling into the backseat.

"¿Adónde va? ¿Celestún?" The driver asks.

I'm taken aback. Although I try to practice Spanish regularly, it's been years since I've spoken it with someone else.

"Yeah...uh, I mean..sí."

"¿Habla español?" he asks and I groan.

"Is everything okay?" Sam whispers from behind his mask.

"He's speaking Spanish," I explain.

"You know Spanish," Sam says with full confidence in me and my abilities. Yeah, I can speak baby Spanish, not well, and that was when I practiced regularly with Luna. Nervousness bubbles around in my belly, and I scrunch my fingers as an outlet.

"I'm not great at it," I admit.

"You're better than you think you are," Sam says, staring at me. God, I'm about to embarrass myself. I interlock Sam's hand with mine and squeeze his fingers before I answer.

"Más o menos."

"Ah!" The driver's face brightens in the rearview mirror. "¿Porqué visitar?"

That's easy. Why am I visiting? Luna!

"Mi amiga...o nuestro amiga," I say looking at Sam.

In the rearview mirror, the driver turns from me to Sam. "Es su novio?"

Mi novio? My cheeks burn, and my eyes widen.

"No, no, no," I rush to say. I release my hand from Sam's. I can see how this looks. "Nosotros...amigos. Solamente amigos."

Sam dips his head towards mine. Concern marks his features. I shake my head. He does *not* need to know what the driver just asked. The driver looks again between Sam and me before shrugging and turning his attention to the road. He turns the radio up. Latin music fills the car. I slide from the middle seat to behind the driver to get further away from Sam. Sticking my hands between my thighs, I only get them out when Sam asks for the water. He's thirsty from having had that milkshake earlier.

We speak little on the hour and a half drive to Celestún. I watch the colorful streets of Mérida turn into forest and eventually beach as the driver turns into our seaside rental. We grab our bags from the trunk and wave goodbye to the driver who says, "I hope you enjoy your vacation with your friends." A smirk dances on his lips.

He's bilingual, and he had me sweating through Spanish. I guess that's what I get for not asking. As he drives away, I shake my head in disbelief then turn towards our rental. It's warm outside although the sun is a couple of hours from setting.

The entrance is reminiscent of a church with its pentagonal shape. The house has a breezeway that lets us see the ocean in the back. It's taking all of my restraint to not rush towards it. I walk up the stairs admiring the palm trees bordering the entrance and run my hands across the rough stucco walls. When we walk inside, I marvel at the two stories and the glass chandelier in the living room.

Luna and Ari come out of the room they picked, and it takes me .2 seconds to see the changes in Luna. She's still a thick girl like me, but it looks like she's growing into her shape. Her wavy hair has brown (probably natural) highlights and her honey brown skin has darkened. She's still beautiful, and tears start welling in my eyes as I rush over to her and hug her. For the last two years, she's been just a face on my screen, but now she's real. I'm holding her. I'm smelling the coconut shampoo she still uses, and now she's wearing some fruity citrusy perfume. It's not too much otherwise I'd be choking, but it feels so good to hold her again. Squeezing her is squeezing my heart.

"And you're Naima," Ari says. Their accent is much thicker than Luna's, but there's also a hint of snark in the back of it.

Still holding onto Luna, I turn my head towards them. "I am," I say, craning my head to lay on Luna's shoulder.

"I heard you latch on," they remark.

I turn to Luna betrayed. Latch on? But she loves my long tight hugs. Sam wraps his arm around my lower back to gently push me aside so he can grab a hug from Luna and introduce himself to Ari.

"How was your flight?" Luna asks.

"We slept for most of it," Sam says.

"So you can party?" Luna raises an eyebrow at him.

"Whatchya got?" he asks.

She walks over to her duffel bag laying on the dining room table and pulls out a pack of gummies.

"Thirty milligrams," she says, dangling the bag. His mouth turns into an O. I'm guessing that's a lot.

"Maybe we can unpack and settle into rooms before y'all do drugs?" I yell from the foyer.

"Take it you're not the stoner type?" Ari asks.

I shrug. Sophomore year, I started experimenting with alcohol, and by experimenting I mean having a hard seltzer for parties. Like one. Sometimes when it's me and Sam, I'd have two, but never enough to get drunk. I'm a little too afraid of losing control.

"Tonight can be the night you start, Princess." Ari bumps their elbow into my arm.

Princess? Already with the nicknames.

I walk around the house. There are four bedrooms: one for Luna and Ari, one for Sam, one for me, and one for my cousin

Eric who's supposed to get here tonight. We booked this place at the beginning of the year. When I saw the photos, it didn't look like this—a mix of coziness and luxury. Plush furniture next to large oversized windows. A pool. The bedrooms are simple with queen beds, two nightstands, and nothing else. Although I will say the colors are a bit bland and dated, I think the fact that it's on the beach is the main draw.

I grab the other downstairs bedroom near the kitchen. Sam grabs one of the bedrooms upstairs. I plop on the bed setting my suitcase and bookbag beside me. Doing a quick body scan, I feel neutral. Not overly bad or good. Not too tired or too excited. I close my eyes, trying to gather myself, and breathe before I have to join the others.

Once I feel settled, I rejoin the group in the small living room. There's a loveseat where Ari and Luna are sitting. Sam is sitting in the armchair on one side of the loveseat so I sit in the opposite one. Sam's talking about his electrician program that he's been in. He just graduated in August and has been looking for a job since. The place he did his apprenticeship hired him part-time once he graduated, but he told me he wants a full time job.

"Have you decided if you're staying in Redbud Springs or not?" Luna asks.

He turns from Luna to me before saying, "I haven't decided yet."

"What if you went to Jackson so you could be with Naima?"

Luna offers.

"That'd be fun. You could come see me after classes," I chime in.

Our freshman year Sam came to visit almost every weekend, but then sophomore year he came a lot less. That was when his apprenticeship started so I understood. Now that he's graduated and could be working set hours, we can hang out more.

"I don't know. We'll see," Sam says.

Luna turns her attention from Sam to me, "How's everything at Millsaps? You said Organic Chem is a nightmare."

"Girl," I say before ranting about how learning anything makes my head hurt and how the professor literally has it out for us. "He acts like he doesn't want us to graduate."

Luna winces, "Sorry."

"What are you going to do with your chemistry major?" Ari asks.

"It's biochem, and I'm working towards being a research scientist. I have an internship next semester for it."

"You got that?" Luna asks.

The last time I talked to her was about a month ago for her birthday, and they told me I got the position a week later, after Thanksgiving break was over when it was time to study for biochem finals. I forgot to update her.

"Yeah," I grimace. "I'm so nervous."

"You'll be fine," Luna reassures me. "You are the smartest person I know, and you're probably ten times better at science than everyone else there."

I reach over Ari to grab Luna's hands, and she reaches out to hold mine. Although it's been two years since I've been able to do this, it's like old times, and I'm still so grateful to have her in my life.

"Is there something you have to tell me?" Ari asks, knocking us out of our trance.

I keep holding one hand, letting go of Luna's other. Ari seems a little possessive of her.

"Eric!" Luna remembers. "When's he getting here?"

"Well Eric's a they now, but they're getting here later. I think their flight left around the same time, but L.A. is an eight hour flight so give them a few hours."

"Well *they* didn't tell me that at our last planning call," Luna pouts.

"I think they're still trying to figure out which pronouns fit, but anyway, Eric is bringing a boy!" I squeal. Eric has never introduced us to any of their partners before, and we finally get to meet one.

"I think I'm gonna grab a beer," Sam says heading for the fridge.

Luna watches him until he leaves the room before asking, "Who is this boy?" She shimmies.

"I have no idea. I wonder if they met in LA."

"Maybe." Luna nibbles her bottom lip, glances towards the kitchen, then asks, "Speaking of boys, what happened with

Isaiah?"

I roll my eyes. Isaiah was a guy who I met in my core classes. In terms of looks, he was alright I guess. Kind of tall, skinny. He constantly had a shaved head which when you have beautiful Black hair, why do you keep cutting it off? We hung out a little bit and around this time last year, he wanted to date. I agreed because it had been almost a year and a half since Kamron and I broke up so why not? But what ensued was four months of awkwardness. I thought we had to just try and find our rhythm but after four months, I gave up.

"Sex with him was horrible," I admit.

Ari chokes and Luna sighs. She smooshes her lips together, and her eyebrows knit together in concern.

"He just rammed it in and was like" — I smack one hand against my fist over and over— "That was the final straw for me."

"Was it over and over or just once?" Luna asks.

"Just once," I say when Ari asks incredulously, "*Over* and *over*?"

"This is why I feel bad for straight women," Ari remarks. "You endure bad sex *multiple* times."

"Well," I shrug. "Everyone has to learn somewhere."

Was my first few times having sex perfect? No, but I had someone who listened to me so it made the experience ten times better than what I did with Isaiah.

Ari reels back like what we're saying is blasphemy.

"It was one time, and he didn't listen to me so I never spoke to him again," I reassure them. "Literally nothing to worry about."

"How is everything holding up?" Luna nods towards my thighs. "You know? Down there?"

"I'm fighting for my life." I recline my head back. "I broke my vibrator a few months ago."

She laughs. "You broke it?!"

"I did," I nod. "I don't think I'm going to make it. I just don't want another Isaiah incident."

As Thee Queen Megan says, sometimes the dick ain't worth coming back for seconds, and I just want something that'll last. I'm not even looking for another Kamron. I just want a guy who's kind, intelligent, handsome, funny, and who listens to me. Someone who's patient and loving. I've had it before, can't I get it again, or is that really too much for the universe?

"Have you talked to Kamron again since his birthday?" Luna asks.

Fireflies dance along my cheeks. Right after the Isaiah incident, I kept thinking about Kamron and how perfect we were together, and when I looked up, it was his birthday, and he asked if we could video call. I said yes immediately and seeing his face again, hearing his voice—my body had a visceral reaction. Since then he's still jetsetting across the world, and I've been crying over Organic Chem, taking breaks only to like all of his pictures and videos like some fangirl.

"No, I haven't," I admit.

I'm not going to say that I'm afraid to talk to him again, but I don't really have a reason to and maybe he's moved on since we dated. Maybe he'll only ever see me as a friend from here on out, and I should be grateful for the time we had together.

"What about you and that guy?" Ari asks, nodding towards the kitchen.

"Sam?" I ask. They can't be serious. I doubt I'd ever want to have sex with Sam. It'd be too weird. He's seen me in a lot of different ways, but I don't know if I want him to see me...in that way.

Luna elbows Ari and they ask, "What? I'm just saying. He's objectively attractive and so are you, and you're both single, right?"

I glance at the kitchen. Sam can't be listening to this right now. What if he is? My cheeks burn. He's going to think *things*. Do I want him to think those things? What if he's already thought it, and it's me who hasn't thought about the things?

Luna waves to catch my attention. "Don't listen to Ari. They're just being a pendejo."

"¿Pendejo?" Ari reels back then launches into rapid-fire angry Spanish.

My attention turns back to the kitchen where Sam could be, but he probably went outside or somewhere else in this giant house. First the driver and now Ari. Why do people always assume we're a couple? Could we be? Have I not noticed that there could be something between us? I mean I had a crush on him when I was twelve, but that was eight years ago. I buried the possibility of that ever happening. Could Sam want me? Romantically?

The crew returns in *Love Me or Leave Me*, the sequel to *Between Us*.